Books by Zoe Burke

The Annabelle Starkey Mysteries
Jump the Gun
No Gun Intended

Children's Books
Lightning Bug Thunder

Charley Harper Board Books
Animal Alphabet
Book of Colors
Count the Birds

arley Harper's Nature Discovery Books
What's in the Coral Reef?
What's in the Rain Forest?
What's in the Woods?

No
Inte

No Gun Intended

An Annabelle Starkey Mystery

Zoe Burke

Poisoned Pen Press

Copyright © 2015 by Zoe Burke

First Edition 2015

10 9 8 7 6 5 4 3 2 1

Library of Congress Catalog Card Number: 2015946349

ISBN: 9781464204845   Hardcover
      9781464204869   Trade Paperback

Poisoned Pen Press
6962 E. First Ave., Ste. 103
Scottsdale, AZ 85251
www.poisonedpenpress.com
info@poisonedpenpress.com

Printed in the United States of America

For Martha, the best sister *ever*

Acknowledgments

At Poisoned Pen Press, heartfelt thanks to Annette Rogers, editor, and Barbara Peters, editor-in-chief, for getting me back on course after I strayed to The Dark Side—and kudos to the rest of the PPP team, all class acts.

I am fortunate to be represented by Anna Olswanger, my agent, who has always advised me well. This time she persuaded me (kicking and screaming) to write a plot summary upfront—which proved to be surprisingly helpful.

My inestimable friend and inspiring writer Bonnie Smetts read my manuscript and cheered me on with her usual insightful suggestions.

California crony Debby Barrall graciously put me in touch with firearms expert Mick Olson and Detective Matthew Barrall. Their willingness to spend time educating me was beyond generous, and the invaluable information they provided bolstered this story as it will future plots. Thank you.

Darius Burke unknowingly contributed an important word to this book, for which I am much obliged.

Almost all of the Portland places mentioned in this book are real, though all but two of the characters are fictitious. I'm lucky to live in such a vibrant and beautiful city.

I am endlessly grateful for the tireless support I receive from my friends and family and for my husband, Thomas, who still slays me, year after year, decade after decade.

Chapter One

I don't sleep on planes. I watch movies. In fact, I don't fly airlines that don't offer free movies. Watching films on my iPad just doesn't do it for me. I'd rather sit back with a glass of wine and be entertained without worrying about my battery going dead. "Airplane mode" for me means I leave all electronic devices tucked away and turned off. Okay, it's not like I'm a jetsetter and have my pick of flights and jumbo-jet myself from coast to coast all the time like George Clooney in *Up in the Air* when his job was to axe employees from companies all over the country. What a life. Good film, though.

Anyway, movies are important to me. I watch them religiously at home, with Bonkers, my cat, on my lap, and Mickey, my boyfriend, snuggled up next to me. On airplanes, movies allow me to forget that I'm 33,000 feet in the air. No one should have to think about that.

This time I was focused on the backseat screen on a night flight from JFK to Portland, Oregon. I was flying business! I never fly business. Mickey upgraded me. He's rich, having inherited a not-so-small fortune from his parents. He thought I was crazy to fly at night, especially since I don't sleep on planes. But it was either leave at eight-thirty in the morning, which would mean getting up at four-thirty in order to shower and make my hair presentable (would that I had Julia Roberts' locks, but mine are more like Keanu Reeves') and make it to JFK in time, or take the six-thirty p.m. flight, which landed me in Portland at ten.

Thanks to Mickey looking out for me, I got dinner, a wide seat with plenty of leg room (which is important for long-legged, big-footed me), and the relief of cinematic distraction.

Mickey drove me to the airport in his Mustang. We rarely use it in New York, where we live on Cornelia Street in the West Village. He keeps it garaged, except for special occasions. I told him I could take a cab. He told me to wear a scarf because he was going to put the top down.

There went my carefully blow-dried hair.

We had a good-bye kiss worthy of cinematic acclaim when he dropped me off in front of the Delta skycap counter. "You'll call me when you land?"

"I will."

"Give my best to the 'rents."

"I will. Kiss me again, like it's your last chance to kick the ball on second down."

"You and your cockeyed sports metaphors. What does that even mean?"

But he lifted me off my feet while pressing his lips against mine, so I guess he figured it out.

A couple of hours later, I had finished my meal of overcooked pasta with tomato sauce, my first glass of cabernet sauvignon, and a too-sweet piece of lemon cake, while riveted to a scene toward the end of *Begin Again*. Keira Knightley and Mark Ruffalo had finished making their indy album on the streets of New York, and I could feel the magnetism between them. I didn't know if they were going to kiss, or if they knew it wouldn't work, and then they parted, and I was glad and sad at the same time.

That's when the guy next to me, who had been sleeping soundly, suddenly woke up with a start, flailing his arm and knocking my second glass of wine off my tray table onto the front of my white sweater.

I ripped off my headphones and tried to jump up, but my seat belt was fastened and the tray table was not stowed since we were not about to land or take off, so I only managed a pitiful little seat jump, my arms up the air like I was about to be arrested.

"Oh, God, what a mess. I'm so sorry." He fumbled around in his suit jacket. Maybe he thought he had a handkerchief or an extra sweater in there.

The wineglass rolled to the floor. "It's okay," I said, but it wasn't okay at all. I looked like I was drenched in blood.

I headed to the teeny tiny airplane bathroom where a flight attendant met me and gave me a can of club soda. "Dump this on the wine. It will help."

I closed the door and latched it, took off the sweater and pushed it into the miniature airplane bathroom sink—keeping the sleeves out—and started pouring. I watched it bubble for a while. Then I looked at myself in the mirror and remembered that I hadn't thought I needed to wear a T-shirt or camisole or anything but my bra underneath. What was I thinking? Why did I decide that traveling in white was a good idea? Did I really still not know how to dress at thirty-three years old?

I rinsed the sweater, wrung the ever-loving crap out of it, and started patting it madly with paper towels. It was now damp all over with a pink splotch on its front that resembled a very large nose. I put it on and regarded myself again in the mirror. I looked like I had been nuzzled by a Siberian tiger, or Bessie the cow.

I tried to smooth down my hair, which had started sticking out in odd patterns, probably due to my headset, and tucked it behind my ping-pong-paddle ears (if ears had sizes, mine would be the same as my feet, ten), and made my way back to my seat. The flight attendants had cleaned up the mess, and my seatmate gave me a somewhat pitiful grimace as I approached.

"May I buy you another glass?"

I sat and fastened my seat belt. "Well, actually, the wine is free, so sure, knock yourself out." I smiled at him.

He scrunched up his face. "How 'bout I buy you a new sweater?"

"I don't think they offer them in the duty-free magazine, but thanks for the offer." I was being a little unkind, so I followed that with, "Really, don't worry. It was an accident. I shouldn't have worn white. Go back to sleep." I gave him another smile and put my headset back on. I had missed the end of *Begin Again*.

I passed on another glass of wine offered by another flight attendant, and set about watching *At Middleton,* where Andy Garcia and Vera Farmiga meet for a day at a college campus and fall in love and have to decide if they'll bail on their disappointing lives or return to them. I won't spoil the ending for you, but it made me teary, while shivering in my damp sweater, so I was glad when the pilot's voice came on the audio system and told us we'd be landing shortly.

Portland had become the new home base for my parents, Jeff and Sylvia Starkey, after violent events of last year had played out in their house in Palo Alto, California. Violent events brought on—through no fault of our own—by Mickey and me. They didn't want to stay in that house any longer. So they sold it and bought a great little 1920s bungalow in the southeast section of Portland. I had been back once before to help with the move, but this would be my first visit since they were really settled.

I had moved to New York to live with Mickey a little over a year ago, when he was still an NYPD detective. He wanted to branch out on his own, and a few weeks ago we finally launched a new detective agency, Asta Investigations. I named it, I'm proud to say, after the dog in *The Thin Man.* It had taken us a while to get all the partnership paperwork in order and for Mickey to take the PI examination required by the state. Our friend Luis, a cop we met in Las Vegas, and his wife, Ruby, were planning on joining us, but so far they hadn't. Mickey didn't want them to make the big change until we had some solid jobs lined up. That would happen soon: Mickey was already on a missing-person case sent his way by a buddy from the NYPD.

As for me, I was in it for Mickey. I was head-over-heels in love with him, and once the new business got rolling, I would help out with research and dumpster diving. In anticipation of this lofty career, I got business cards made for all of us. Mine is printed with my name, Beatrice Annabelle Starkey, followed by "DDS." That "S" is for "specialist." Anyway, so far I had been spending my time enjoying New York and getting back in shape after a period of leisure, trying to regain my strength and confidence following the previously noted violent events. But it was time for me to get off the couch and find something productive to do. It was also time for me to visit my parents in their new home.

They met me at the airport, Mom waving her arms wildly as soon as she saw me walking into the general lobby area. "Honey! Here we are!" Dad stood beside her with his gentle grin expanding into a full-fledged beaming smile.

I wrapped my arms around them and kissed each of them. "I'm so glad to be here."

"We've missed you, Bea," said Dad.

"Damn, goddamn straight, we have," added Mom, never one to mince words.

We took the escalator down to baggage claim. Dad said he'd bring the car around outside while Mom and I waited for my suitcase. I wrestled my arms out of my backpack and dropped it by my feet.

"What's that?" Mom asked, pointing at the backpack.

"Um, Mom, it's the backpack you and Dad gave me...?"

"No shit, honey. I mean that thing tied on it."

I laughed. "Mickey gave me that, for good luck. It's a sterling silver cricket, tied onto my zipper pull. Crickets stop chirping when danger is near. They're protectors."

I shivered.

"Darling, are you cold?"

I turned to Mom and opened my jacket. "Cold and damp."

"Holy shit, Annabelle, is that blood?" Mom leaned in for a closer look while I smiled sweetly at the couple standing next to us, who clearly had a no-swearing rule in their house.

"Chill, Mom! It's wine. The guy next to me on the plane doused me."

And suddenly he was right there, handing me some cash. Two bills, a twenty and a five, to be precise. "Hello. Please take this and buy yourself a new sweater."

Okay, I'm no fashion queen, but this was cheap, I thought, for replacing my sweater, even though I bought it on sale at H&M.

"No, honestly, it's all right, I think I can save it with some more club soda." That was the first time I really looked at him. He was only about five-foot nine or ten, just a few inches taller than me. A little chunky, but with a sweet face and thick white hair. Probably in his fifties. He was wearing an expensive tailored suit. I could tell, since Mickey was a snappy dresser himself.

Mr. Dapper was insistent, practically shoving the money at me while looking at my mother. "Loren Scranton. Nice to meet you." He held out his other hand to her.

She shook it. "Mr. Scranton. I'm Sylvia Starkey and this is my daughter, Annabelle." She nodded at me. "It's very nice of you to pay for the sweater."

I hesitated to take the money, but I did since he was pushing it at me and Mom seemed to think I should. "Thank you, really."

"Do you live in Portland, Mr. Scranton?" asked Mom.

"Please, call me Loren."

They started chatting amiably about things that strangers chat amiably about. I didn't stick around. I saw my suitcase heading out of the shoot and went to retrieve it.

When I got back to Mom, Scranton had left. "He doesn't live here. He lives in New York. Nice guy. He felt awful about your sweater."

I snorted. "Not *that* awful. I mean, twenty-five dollars?"

We started heading outside. "Well, darling, it's not a very nice-looking sweater."

"You should have seen it when it was all white."

It was early November, and it was cold, in the thirties. There was a good chance of snow during the night. The rain already fell heavily. We rushed into the house from the car and stomped our feet on the welcome mat. Dusty, their golden retriever, wiggled like crazy while we all petted her. Dad took my backpack and suitcase upstairs while I dumped my coat on the bench by the front door.

"Tired, honey, or do you want a drink?" Mom was heading toward the kitchen.

"Both. How about a bourbon nightcap."

She started pulling down the glasses and a lovely looking bottle I had never seen before. "What is that?"

"Angel's Envy. Don't you love the name? And the bottle? I bought it just for you. Couldn't resist."

She poured me one, and a glass of wine for herself, and a scotch for Dad. He came downstairs and we all sat in the living room, them on the couch, me on the recliner, and Dusty at Dad's feet.

"So, how's the new job going, Mom? And what are you up to anyway, Dad? The last we talked you were working a lot on the house?"

Dad sipped his drink and nodded. "Yes, and enjoying it, muffinhead." Dad had always called me that, ever since I could remember, in spite of my protestations. "Painting, installing some bookshelves upstairs in our bedroom. Planning on redoing the downstairs bathroom next."

"It's enough? Being Mr. Handyman?" Dad was an astrophysicist and had taken a sabbatical from Stanford University, where he had taught for many years.

"You know, right now, it is. We'll see how it goes."

"Your father, Annabelle, is a genius. Well, we already knew that, but he can figure out how to build anything, for chrissakes! It's amazing that I didn't know this about you, darling!" Mom leaned over and gave Dad a kiss. He put his arm around her.

"And you, Mom?" Mom had left her job as an emergency-room doctor in California and had started working at a hospital just outside of Portland.

"I'm fine dear, still feeling my way…"

"Sylvia, just tell her." Dad gave her a squeeze.

"Tell me what?! What's wrong?!"

Mom took a big swig of wine and set her glass down. "I lost the job at the clinic. Only lasted six months."

"Huh? How is that possible?"

She shook her head. "I swore at a patient."

"They fired *you* for *swearing?*"

Dad tilted his head toward me. "Well, it was more complicated than that."

Mom sighed. "The patient was president of the hospital board. He's a dickhead. He was in emergency because he thought he was dying, but he really just had the flu. I told him so, and he said he wanted all sorts of tests done, and I insisted they were unnecessary, and he said he didn't care, he'd pay for them, and I said he should go home and rest instead, and he said that it was his decision, and that if I were a good doctor, I would do what he wanted, not to mention he was the president of the board, and I told him to go fuck himself, because I was busy."

I couldn't help but laugh.

"Oh, honey, it's not very funny. I was called before the board the following week, and one by one, they pissed me off, and I'm afraid I told them all to go fuck themselves. And, here we are." She rolled her eyes and swallowed some more wine.

Dad put his feet up on the ottoman. "She had a contract, that's the thing, and we're trying to decide what to do next. They can claim that Sylvia didn't behave professionally, but I'm not sure this incident is grounds to fire her. On the other hand, she's not sure she wants to work there after this, are you, honey?"

Mom shook her head. "No, I'm considering other occupations. Like training cadaver dogs."

I sat up straight. "Huh? You mean dogs that find dead people?"

Mom laughed. "I saw a special on television about them. Pretty impressive. But I'm also considering opening a bakery, or running for mayor, or becoming a plumber." She laughed again. "I don't know what the hell I'm doing, Bea."

I stood up and went over to her and kissed the top of her head. "Well, I vote for the dogs. You're a terrible cook, you couldn't win an election with that potty mouth of yours, and I think plumbing pipes are a lot different from the human kind."

Dad stood up, too. "Going to bed?"

"Yup, I'm whupped. See you in the morning." I gulped the rest of my bourbon, coughed, hugged him, and headed upstairs.

My parents' guest room is one of the sweetest rooms in the whole world. The walls are painted a lovely butter-yellow, and the double bed is cushy, covered with a duvet that's as warm as a hot bath and as light as a cloud. I knelt on the large hooked rug that covered most of the wide-plank wood floor and unzipped my suitcase, pulling out my flannel PJs and my toiletry kit.

Then I reached for my backpack to pull out my contacts case and glasses.

The cricket wasn't there.

"Damn," I swore, thinking it must have fallen off when Mom was tossing it into the trunk.

I unzipped it and reached into the front compartment.

And froze.

My hand closed around the metal handle of what felt like a gun.

I pulled it out to be certain.

I don't know much about guns. In fact, I only know about two of them. Mickey has a Glock, and I have a Beretta Nano. Mickey had bought it for me about a month earlier. It's pink. I know, a cutesy color. He picked it out as part of his effort to convince me to own a gun and learn how to use it. But I'm uneasy around guns. We never had one in our house while I was growing up, and I never knew anyone who had a gun—until I met Mickey. So my pink one was still in a box in our closet at home.

This gun in my hand wasn't a Glock or a Nano.

I dropped it on the bed and dug further into the backpack. It wasn't mine.

It sure as hell looked like mine: Columbia logo, black.

But the only thing in it was the gun and a poufy jacket, which filled out the main compartment nicely.

What the hell?

Mom must have picked this up by mistake while I got my suitcase off the baggage claim carousel.

So, who owned this gun, and where was my backpack?

I sat on the edge of the bed, took a deep breath, and called Mickey.

"Hey! You okay?" he answered.

"Mickey. I have a gun in a backpack that isn't mine."

"What are you talking about?"

So I told him, and he told me to call the police right away, and I did.

I left the gun and the backpack on the bed, went downstairs, and waited for the cops to show up.

My parents were going to be so sorry I came for a visit.

Chapter Two

It was a little past midnight when the doorbell rang. Dusty barked, and I opened the door to two men in suits flashing badges.

"Ms. Starkey?"

"Yes. Please come in."

"Detectives Monroe and Dawson."

I held out my hand to each of them, and they removed their gloves to shake, while Dusty wiggled up against their legs. Dawson squatted beside her to give her some good pets. I liked him.

Monroe immediately started scouting my parents' living room and took out his notebook. I didn't like him so much.

I've got nothing against the police. I fell in love with a police detective, after all. But I've met some bad ones, so I'm quick to size them up. Trust my gut. Tread carefully.

"Detectives, huh? I figured a uniform would respond."

"We were in the vicinity. Got the call."

"Where's the gun?" Dawson asked.

"GUN? What the hell is going on here?" Mom had appeared at the foot of the stairs in her bathrobe. Dad was on his way down.

"Mom, Dad, meet detectives Monroe and Dawson. I found a gun in my backpack and called the police. I mean, someone else's backpack." Dawson stood up.

Mom froze, speechless, possibly for the first time in her life. Dad moved in front of her. "How is that possible, Bea?"

I shook my head. "Bad luck, Dad. It seems to follow me around like we're in a Marx Brothers skit together." I motioned toward the stairs and addressed the cops. "Upstairs. Follow me." They did, with Dad and Mom right behind them, and Dusty bringing up the rear.

We all crowded into the guest room, and I pointed to the gun and backpack. Mom sat on the bed. "Oh, fuck, Annabelle. Was it that guy? Scranton?"

Dawson put on one of his gloves and picked up the gun. Monroe considered Mom, and then me. "Scranton?"

"Loren Scranton. Sat next to me on the plane. Spilled wine on me. Saw us in baggage claim and gave me twenty-five bucks for my sweater—and I'm sorry, but that was just too Franklin Harty for me, if you know what I mean." I pointed at my stained sweater, lying in a heap on the floor. Dawson and Monroe frowned. Clearly they didn't know what I meant. "The boss played by Dabney Coleman in *9 to 5*?! He was rich and miserly."

"How do you know that Scranton is rich?" Monroe asked, regarding my sweater.

"Fancy suit. Anyway, Mom, he was talking to either you or me the whole time. Did you see him pick up my backpack?"

Mom shook her head.

Monroe was scouting out the guest room like it was a safe house for terrorists. "The backpack most probably was dropped from someone coming into baggage claim from outside the airport. It couldn't have passed through security unless a TSA guy was asleep on the job." His eyes came around and rested on me. "Maybe this someone wanted to give you this gun for some reason?"

My gut was right. I didn't like this guy. "Believe me, no one would want to give *me* a gun. I mean, my boyfriend already did, and that hasn't worked out so well." As soon as I said that, I was sorry.

Monroe took a step toward me. "Your boyfriend?"

I sighed. "Yes, Mickey, my partner in New York, he's a detective. He bought me one recently. Beretta Nano, for protection. But I haven't used it. Well, just once at a firing range, but I hated it, so it's in a box in the closet."

"Do you or Mickey know anyone in Portland?" Dawson asked.

"No. No one except my parents, and they haven't lived here that long." I watched Dawson return the gun to the backpack and pick it up. "Um, by the way, what kind of gun is that?" I wanted to tell Mickey.

"It's a Beretta Bobcat."

"Wow! They make Bobcats *and* Nanos? They've got someone with a sense of humor in their marketing department!" I flashed a big smile at Dawson and then Monroe to no effect, and then tried it on Mom and Dad, whose pained expressions did not change.

Monroe suggested that we all go downstairs to the living room, where he could get our names and contact information, so we did. After about thirty minutes, they stood up to leave. "Ms. Starkey, you're not leaving town soon, I hope?"

"No, but what do you mean by that? Do you think I have something to do with this? Because I..."

"Just in case we have more questions, or need you to identify any pictures, anything like that," Dawson interrupted me. "We'll see if we can find the owner based on the serial number. We'll check it for prints, too." He smiled.

"Okay. I understand." I sort of understood. Mostly I was thinking about my missing contact lens case, glasses, and Denise Mina's recent mystery, not to mention a lucky cricket. At least I still had my wallet and my Kate Hepburn biography in my purse. "Do you think someone will turn my backpack in to lost-and-found at the airport, or to a police station?"

Monroe and Dawson didn't say anything in response, just gave me a "gee, we're sorry" look, and turned to go. "Let us know if you leave the area."

Dad opened the door for them. "Thank you, detectives. Will you let us know what you find out?"

Dawson nodded. "Thanks, folks."

And they were gone.

Mom was still amazingly quiet, sitting on the couch. Dad shut the door and came to me to give me a hug. "It's just a weird, random act, muffinhead. You were in the right place at the wrong time." He took my face in his hands. "I wish I hadn't left to go park the car." He kissed my forehead.

"Dad, this is not your fault. No one's fault. Let's try to forget all about it and go to bed." I turned to Mom. "Right, Mom? Ready to get some sleep?"

Mom came out of her stupor and just about leapt to her feet. "Sleep? Sure. Forget about it? No. We're going to find Loren Scranton and I'm going to give him a piece of my mind and a kick in his balls with the toe of the cowboy boots I just bought."

"Sylvia, that's absolutely not what you're going to do. The police will handle this." Dad held his hand out to her. "Come on to bed."

Mom shifted her eyes from me to Dad and back again. "Well, they better figure it out. I won't have my daughter mixed up with criminals and cops again." She kissed my cheek as she passed me. "See you in the morning, dear."

They retreated upstairs and I collapsed in the recliner, pulling my phone out of my pocket to give Mickey an update. I shook my head. When did my mother become a vigilante? And since when did she wear cowboy boots? And what color were they? I love cowboy boots.

Chapter Three

Portland has the reputation of being deluged by constant rain, but that's a myth perhaps perpetuated by residents who wish to keep its charms a secret from possible invaders from too-expensive California. My first morning poured bright sunlight and blue skies through the bedroom windows. I peeked outside at the giant sequoia in my parents' backyard. It hadn't snowed after all. I could hear some construction noises and espied a huge crane on nearby Division Street. Dad had told me that a mess of new apartment buildings and retail shops were going up.

I rolled out of bed, smoothed my flannel pajamas and pulled up my wool socks, combed my hair and stuck it behind my ears, and brushed my teeth. I popped in my lenses, which I had stored in an old case of Mom's I found in the bathroom, and ambled downstairs. Mom was pouring a cup of coffee and humming along to an old Joni Mitchell album that was playing in the den. My parents still listen to vinyl. They've got a closet full of 33s. A veritable library of old rock 'n' roll, as well as jazz and classical stuff. But Joni, well, she's Mom's BFF in make-believe land.

She handed me the cup. "Morning, honey! How'd you sleep?"

"Great. Thanks." I took a sip. "Aaah. Coffee cake?"

She smiled. "Of course. From a bakery on Division. I'll cut you a piece."

I sat at the dining room table and took a brief look at the front page of the *Oregonian,* then opted to gaze out the window instead. A squirrel ran along the top of the backyard fence and up the trunk of the mammoth tree. This was like living in the city and the country, all at once.

Mom joined me, putting a plate with a serving of coffee cake in front of me. "Eat up."

I picked it up with my hands and took a bite. "Yum. This is delish."

"Don't talk while you're eating." She leaned on the table with her forearms. "What shall we do today?"

I swallowed. "Whatever you want. Where'd you buy your cowboy boots, and what color are they? Maybe we could go get some more."

Mom laughed. "Green! A cool little store in the Pearl District. Sure, we can do that. But, it's such a gorgeous day, I thought we'd go to the Japanese Garden. It has become one of our favorite places in Portland. I can't wait to show it to you."

I took another bite and gave her a thumbs-up.

"I looked him up, by the way," Mom said.

I swallowed again. "Who?"

"Loren Scranton."

I leaned back in my chair. "Mom! Who are you, Lis Salander? Are you hacking into computers now?"

"Who's Lis Salander?"

"*The Girl with the Dragon Tattoo*. Didn't you see that movie? Or read the book? Good stuff."

Mom shook her head. "No. Anyway, all I did was Google him." She paused. "Want to know what I found out?"

"Not really." We stared at each other. "Go ahead. Tell me."

Mom grinned and jumped up to get a notepad from the kitchen counter, then came back to sit down with me. "He's an accountant!"

"Dangerous guy. Wow."

"And he lives in Brooklyn!"

"We'd better alert the *New York Times*."

"And, best of all…" She paused again for effect.

"Please, Mom, I can't stand this suspense. Wait, don't tell me. He's a Boy Scout leader!"

Mom snorted. "No! He's a member of the NRA!"

I laughed. "So are about a billion other people. C'mon, with a name like Loren, I bet he needs a gun to defend himself against bullies."

Mom dropped her notepad on the table. "Well, he probably owns at least one gun, if he's a member. I think that's an important clue."

I rubbed my eyes. "Mom, hell, I own a gun, sort of. That doesn't make me a criminal."

"I know, I know. And we should talk about that some more, I think. It was news to me that Mickey got you a gun. But right now I feel like I'm onto something with this Scranton prick. Maybe something important." She chewed on her lower lip. "Maybe I could volunteer to help out at the police station. Do research or something."

I stood up. "Prick? You don't know that. Well, you sort of do. I mean, a rich guy offering twenty-five bucks for a sweater is a true sign of prickdom. Anyway, slow down, Miss Marple."

She frowned.

"Really, Mom? Agatha Christie? She wrote a ton of mysteries. You should see *4:50 from Paddington*. That movie is a classic. The TV series *Murder, She Wrote* was based on a movie that was based on the first film, and…"

"Annabelle, darling, I have heard of Agatha Christie and Miss Marple, believe it or not. But I don't see why I shouldn't try to help out, and I think you should tell Mickey what I found out about Mr. Scranton."

I nodded. "Yup, he probably wouldn't have already checked him out." I smiled.

Mom rolled her eyes. "Okay, I get it. I'll leave Scranton the dickhead alone for now and you get ready to go to the Japanese Garden."

"Where's Dad?"

"Outside, in front, raking leaves." She put my coffee mug and plate in the sink. "He called the airport, by the way, to inquire about your backpack. No one turned it in."

"Big surprise."

I skipped up the stairs two at a time and took a shower and blow-dried my hair. I got dressed and had just finished putting on a dark blue beret when my phone rang. I didn't recognize the number, but answered right away. "Hello?"

A quiet female voice answered. "Is this Dr. Starkey?" She sounded young.

"No, this is her daughter. Who is this?"

"I'm looking for the dentist, Beatrice Annabelle Starkey?"

Dentist? I thought. "Well, I'm Annabelle, but I'm no dentist. Who is this?"

"Your card says Beatrice Annabelle Starkey, DDS."

I laughed. "That's for Dumpster Diving Specialist. Are you calling from New York?"

"You're a detective?"

I sat on the bed. "Look, you need to tell me who you are and where you got my card…" I stopped. I remembered. I had business cards in my backpack. "My backpack. You found it?"

She paused. "Yes."

"I need it."

"Yes. I will give it to you. But I need the other backpack."

So, what to do. Tell her I didn't have it, tell her the police had it, pretend I didn't know what she was talking about? I opted for the last. "What other backpack?"

"We switched them, right? Don't you have mine?"

"Nope. Just thought someone stole mine at the airport."

I heard her take a deep breath. "Oh, no." Her voice was trembling. "What am I going to do?"

"What's your name?"

"Claudia."

"Claudia, let's meet. You can give me my backpack, and I'll reward you. How about that?"

Now she was crying. "I need more than money."

"Like what?"

"Your help. I need a detective."

Now it was my turn to take a deep breath. "Let's meet. I'm about to visit the Japanese Garden. Can you get there? I can be at the entrance in ninety minutes. Will that work?"

She squeaked out a "yes."

"Bring my backpack, too, right?"

Another squeak, and she hung up.

I'm not a real detective, and I know the first thing I should have done was call Dawson or Monroe and tell them about Claudia. But I wanted to meet her first. Maybe she didn't deserve to be in trouble with the police, whatever trouble she was in. Maybe she was just a kid who got herself into some tight spot. And maybe I wanted to prove to myself—and to my parents and Mickey—that I was back on my feet, strong and able, and ready to meet the world, fearless.

I could see why the Japanese Garden had become a favorite retreat for my parents. Positioned at the top of a hill, its design is exquisite, with meandering paths—stone, wooden, gravel— weaving around ponds and in and out of groves of trees, with benches placed in perfect positions for observing, reading, sketching, meditating. It wasn't crowded at all, being a Monday morning. A gallery building, with a deck providing views of a huge Zen garden as well as downtown Portland, featured work by Isamu Noguch. I had never heard of him before, but his sculptures were as soothing to me as the Japanese maples.

We visited the gift shop and I bought Mickey and me some chopsticks with rabbits on them. We like to get Chinese takeout in New York.

We were starting down the steep path out of the garden back to the car, when I told Mom and Dad I had left my debit card in the shop, and that they should keep going and I'd catch up. It was a ruse, but this way I could meet Claudia on my own.

I hustled back up to the garden entrance, looking around for a girl with my backpack. I checked my watch. She was only about five minutes late, but I couldn't hang around for much longer without Mom and Dad worrying what happened to me.

I pulled out my phone to call her. But as I was about to tap her number on the incoming calls log, I saw Dad hurrying up the path toward me.

"Bea! Quick! Your mother…go help her. I'm going to let the park people know. We've called an ambulance. Someone's hurt." And he ran by me.

I raced down the hill on the curvy path through the thickly wooded evergreens, panting with the effort as well as with increasing dread. I careened around a hairpin turn and stopped short when I saw Mom, kneeling over someone lying in the woods. "Mom! What is it?"

"A young woman." She was tending to her, stanching some bleeding with her scarf. "Hold this here, will you? Someone assaulted her, clobbered her head."

I crouched next to Mom and pressed the scarf against the wound, while Mom took her pulse.

"Is she alive?"

Mom nodded.

Then something caught my eye.

A sparkle, lit by a sunbeam.

It was my silver cricket, perched on my backpack, just a few feet down the hill.

Chapter Four

"Mickey, there's no need for you to come out here. I'm fine. I'm creeped out, but I'm fine." I took a sip of pinot gris. I was sitting on the back porch with my jacket zipped all the way up, gloves on, and my sock-monkey knit hat covering my ears. It's the warmest hat I own and I think it's cute, no matter what Mickey says. Or my mother. As for Dad, he's mute on the monkey-hat debate.

"Babe, I can tell you're upset. Your voice has a weird vibrato going on."

"It's cold and I'm outside."

"Are you wearing your sock-monkey?"

I laughed. "Of course I am. You miss me, right?"

"Especially in that hat. Look, you keep me posted. I want to know what they find out about the girl and the gun. I…" He stopped.

"You what?" I could imagine Mickey running his hand through his dark hair and closing his eyes tight, like he does before he's going to say something he doesn't want to say.

"I'm worried that you're in danger."

I sighed. "No, Claudia's in danger. Not me. Plus, Mom and Dad and Dusty are taking good care of me. You should have seen Mom with Claudia. She was amazing, of course. Took charge of the situation, told me and Dad what to do, gave the EMTs a detailed report on Claudia's pulse and…"

"See? You're upset. You already told me all of this. I'm coming out."

I stamped my feet. My toes were going numb. "No. You have a job. An important one. Any progress on the missing boy? The parents must be frantic."

"Actually, I have a couple of leads." He paused. "I should follow this through, you're right. Every hour that passes reduces the chances of finding this kid, Matthew. But…"

"Let's take this day by day. If I really need you, I'll let you know. Right now, I need to get warm."

Mickey exhaled. "Hmm. I should be getting you warm, in bed."

"That would be nice, but not necessary because I brought…"

"Let me guess: your flannel pajamas?"

"Yup."

"Are you wearing sock-monkey to bed, too?"

I giggled. "That's a little kinky, Mickey, and no. Just big socks on my feet. So, you see, I'm well taken care of."

"You don't need me."

I paused. "I always need you, more than a coach needs his cleats. And I always have you with me, whether you're in bed with me or not."

"Quarterback, you nut. Love you."

"Love you."

We hung up.

I didn't like lying to Mickey, but I didn't want to worry him. Fact was, I *could* be in danger. Claudia was still unconscious, in a coma. Whoever wanted that gun was still out there somewhere, and if Claudia told him or her about our conversation, maybe he or she wasn't too happy about a "detective" being involved. But I wasn't going to alarm Mickey. Not yet, anyway. I was going to play it cool, calm, and collected.

Not an easy role for me. It would be like Chelsea Handler playing the lead in a biopic about Mother Teresa.

Mom had picked up pizza from an Italian restaurant a couple of blocks away, and Dad had thrown together a salad. We sat down to eat, with Dusty eyeing us hopefully.

"How's Mick?" asked Dad.

"Fine. Busy with a case."

"That's good, right?"

"Yup. Good for him. For us. A missing ten-year-old, though, which makes it tough. He said he has some leads, though."

"Well, if anyone can find him, I bet Mickey can," Dad said.

I took a bite of pizza. I had never heard of Brussels sprouts on pizza before, but this was delicious. Béchamel sauce, onions… yum. "This is so good!"

Mom nodded. "Our favorite." She took a swallow of wine. "So, what are we going to do?

"Tomorrow?" I asked.

"No, about the girl."

Dad put his forkful of salad back on its plate. "Syl, what are you talking about? This is in the hands of the police. There is nothing for us to do. We gave our statements, and that's that." He eyed me sternly. "You should have told the police right away that Claudia called you."

"You're right, Dad." I took another bite, not wanting to continue that conversation. The police had already chastised me. But I had every intention of finding out more about Claudia and what happened to her—without the help of Mom's new Nancy Drew alter ego. I couldn't put my parents through any more trauma.

I swallowed and gulped down some water. "Let's not think about this anymore. How about we go shopping tomorrow, Mom? Boots?"

Mom sighed. "Fine. But not until the afternoon. I'm volunteering at the homeless clinic in the morning, eight to twelve."

"Wow! That's wonderful. You didn't tell me!"

"Your mother, Bea, is a godsend doctor there. It's a great clinic, offering free medical exams and treatment." Dad reached over and squeezed Mom's shoulder.

"I mostly take blood pressure and temperatures. But I like it. I've met some great people."

I smiled. "You rock, Mom."

After we finished our meals, I cleared the table and did the dishes. Mom and Dad were reading in the living room, and I joined them with my Hepburn biography. Mom soon declared she was going to bed and kissed us each good night.

Dad leaned toward me. "She's a little rattled."

"I'm sorry, Dad."

"Not your fault, darling. But I want to help you find out what's going on."

I laughed. "What about 'this is in the hands of the police'?"

He smiled. "I'm a good husband."

"You are indeed. But Dad, I don't want either of you involved. Mickey would agree with me on that point, absolutely. He doesn't want any of us to do anything about this."

"He's a good boyfriend." Dad sat back. "But what harm will a little research do?"

We regarded each other for a moment. "Fine," I said. "But just research."

"Good. I'll meet you at the dining-room table in the morning at eight-thirty, with my laptop powered up." He stood up and held out his arms to hug me, and I embraced him.

Chapter Five

I didn't sleep well. Fact was, my flannel PJs and heavy socks weren't very comforting. I missed Mickey more than I thought I would after only a couple of days away from him. I don't like to think that I need him *so* much that I can't function well on my own. But we hadn't been apart since I moved to New York, and the double bed in Portland felt too big, even though it was smaller than our queen-size at home. Joni Mitchell's song about the bed too wide and the frying pan too big rang in my head. I decided to give up on sleep and went downstairs to see if there were any good movies on TV.

It turned out that *The Heat* was just starting, with Melissa McCarthy and Sandra Bullock, and it was just what I needed. I laughed out loud, especially when McCarthy vamps on her captain not having any balls. Dusty slept at my feet, but would wag her tail each time I laughed.

I made my way back to bed at the end and crawled in with a smile on my face. It wasn't long before I was asleep.

It wasn't long before I woke up again, either. Dad was knocking on the door. "Bea, it's eight-thirty."

I sat up. "Right! Coming!" I got up and pulled the afghan on the bed around my shoulders.

Dad had a cup of coffee waiting for me on the table. He was squinting at his laptop screen, scrolling through some Google search, and slurping his own coffee. "Sleep well?"

"Once I got to sleep." I sat down, sipped some coffee, and warmed my hands around the mug. "It's chilly this morning."

Dad didn't look at me. "I can turn up the heat." I noticed he was wearing a fleece pullover. "I don't know how to do Facebook."

"Huh?"

"Claudia Bigelow. I Googled her, and it looks like she's on Facebook, but I can't seem to get anywhere without being a member. I'm on some page, but I can't get anywhere else…"

I peered over his shoulder. "Log in with my e-mail." Dad typed. "Now my password, which is MakeMyDay. Capitalize the first letters and make it all one word."

Dad laughed. "Eastwood. Even I know that one. *Dirty Harry.*" He typed and hit Enter, and a few options for Claudia Bigelow popped up. We identified her right away through her picture, and clicked through to her "about" page.

"Seattle area, lives with her parents, going to community college, twenty years old." I swallowed some more coffee. "Go to her Timeline, Dad."

She had recently posted a few pictures of herself with girl-friends. Dad scrolled down and stopped at the first text entry. It was dated four days ago. "Excited about my trip to Portland. Voodoo donuts and food truck heaven!"

I leaned back. "Translation, Dad?"

"Gourmet doughnuts are a trend here, and the food trucks are known for their quality. Many ethnic varieties. There's a fairly new court of them on Division. We'll treat you while you're here." He paused, still squinting at the screen. "Do you think these pictures with her friends were taken in Portland?"

I scanned the dates. "No. They're dated the same as her Port-land entry, see there?" I pointed.

Claudia wasn't a big Facebooker, so we didn't find out much more, except that she liked "The Voice" and "So You Think You Can Dance" TV shows. We reviewed her list of friends, but that was disappointing, too. Only thirteen, which included her mother, Nancy; and some cousins; as well as said girlfriends in the pictures. There were no boyfriend pictures.

"Maybe she's a lesbian," I mused.

Dad scribbled her mother's name on a notepad and then clicked on her picture. There was even less information there. "I bet she joined Facebook just to keep track of her daughter."

"And I bet that's why her daughter doesn't post much on Facebook." I finished my coffee and got up to pour myself another mugful. "Let's find their street address in Seattle, just in case we want to contact Claudia's parents." I gave Dad a couple of sites to try, and he typed away while I slurped. Mickey had started training me in using the Internet to track people down.

"Got it. That is, if Nancy Bigelow is married to Phillip Bigelow." He wrote down the information and sat back. "Not sure what else we should do. You?"

I shrugged. "Not sure, either. Let's hope Claudia wakes up from that coma soon."

"Breakfast? Eggs?"

"If you're cooking, I'm eating. I'll take a quick shower."

And with that, I trotted upstairs, groggy in spite of the coffee, to make myself presentable. Halfway up, Dad's voice stopped me.

"Bea! Come here!"

I scampered back down. Dad was staring at the computer screen with a smile on his face. "Nice photographs!"

I took a look. He was on *my* Facebook page, scrolling through pictures of me and Mickey. "Dad, you've seen some of those before, I e-mail them to you sometimes...."

He frowned. "You don't have very many Friends."

I sighed. "Dad, it's just Facebook. I don't use it much."

He was scrolling away. "Aha! So that's Ruby!" He had clicked on a picture of Luis' wife. "She's beautiful. When are they moving to New York?"

"We hope by the end of January." I rested my hands on his shoulders. "Um, Dad, could we leave Facebook alone?"

He turned to me. "What's the matter, honey? Something here you don't want me to see?" He smiled. "Why don't I join and we can be friends?"

"Cut it out. You're already my best friend." I leaned over him and closed the browser. "Eggs." I kissed the top of his head and went back upstairs, making a mental note to change my Facebook password. It's not like I had anything to hide, but I didn't want my parents all over my life, either.

The Pearl District in Portland is hip and fun. It used to be the industrial area of downtown, but now it hosts a ton of restaurants, bars, stores, and condos. Mom and I took the bus downtown, and then walked north several blocks to the upscale shoe store where she bought her boots. It was another cold, sunny day, and I was wearing my sock-monkey hat in spite of Mom's objections. A little boy in the store couldn't take his eyes off of me. I smiled at him. He pointed at my head and said, "That hat is for kids."

Mom nodded. "What a smart boy, you are! Doesn't she look silly?"

He nodded back. "Silly."

I rolled my eyes and turned to examine a pair of gray suede boots with contrasting blue accents on the toes and around the backs of the heels. "Wow. These would put Katharine Ross to shame."

"And she is…?" Mom picked up the boot.

"Butch Cassidy and the Sundance Kid."

"Right. Try it on?" She handed it to me.

I peered at the price. "Um, better not." I showed Mom. "Two hundred and fifty buckaroos. And I'm not even employed." I put the boot back on the shelf. "Shore is purty, though."

"That's not a lot for a great pair of boots that will last you a long time."

"Too much for me right now."

Mom smiled. "Good to see that you are budget-aware, my darling. How about I buy you lunch?"

Mom took me to the Byways Café, a small retro diner, and we ordered grilled cheese sandwiches and chocolate milkshakes.

Mom's a doctor, but she doesn't believe in depriving herself or her family of fatty foods on occasion, thank goodness.

We munched away and she asked me about the gun. "I just don't understand why Mickey bought it for you. Is your new life in New York so dangerous that you need it?"

"He simply believes in guns, Mom. I mean, we do have this detective agency now, which means we might be dealing with some criminals from time to time, and Mickey wants me to be prepared."

"I suppose they're necessary. We have friends who have guns, but I just don't fucking like them." Mom grabbed a French fry and stuck it in her mouth, then another, and another.

"I'm not crazy about them, either. You know that. Mine is in the closet. It's probably the main disagreement Mickey and I have about anything." I watched her going at the French fries. "Mom, slow down."

She swallowed and took a sip of her milkshake. "I'm going to the ladies' room."

I sat staring out the window onto Glisan Street, thinking about that gun, and wishing it wasn't in the closet at home, when I focused on someone outside and froze, French fry halfway to my mouth.

It was Loren Scranton. He was peering in the window.

He didn't seem to recognize me, or at least he pretended not to.

I still had on the sock-monkey hat. A good disguise.

I threw some money on the table, put on my jacket and grabbed my purse and Mom's coat and made my way back to the restrooms.

Mom was inside, washing her hands. "Ready to go, dear?"

There was no exit out the back that I could see. I didn't want to alarm Mom, but I didn't want to run into Scranton, either. Was he following us? This was too much of a coincidence to believe that it was a coincidence. "The universe is rarely so lazy," as Benedict Cumberbatch as Sherlock Holmes once said.

"Not quite. Wait for me here?" I handed her our stuff, went into a stall, and latched the door. My heart was racing. If I could delay our exit for a few minutes, maybe Scranton would be far enough away once we left.

"Annabelle, let's head back into downtown. I want to take you to John Helmer's."

I flushed the toilet. "What's that?"

"Mostly men's clothes and hats, but they have a great selection of women's hats, too. I want to buy you one. That monkey of yours has to go."

I came out of the stall. "Okay. Long walk?"

She nodded. "Yes."

"How about a cab?" I figured Scranton would have a hard time tailing us if he was on foot and we weren't.

"For chrissakes, dear, it's a beautiful day and the last I knew, you were running in Central Park every morning. We'll walk. It'll be good for both of us." She put on her coat and handed me my purse. "Buck up, little missy."

I smiled at her weakly. "Mom, I have something to tell you."

She scowled at me. "What?"

"Scranton. He was outside a minute ago. I think he's following us."

She stared at me. "Should we call the police?"

"Let's call a cab, instead." I pulled out my phone. "It's probably just a coincidence."

"Coincidence my ass, Annabelle." She yanked on the door.

"Mom! Where are you going?"

"Outside. I want to find that dickhead."

She left me no choice. I followed her.

She was walking fast and muttering to herself. "That fucking creep. I'll show him a thing or two. Tailing us around like some jackshit stalker. He doesn't know what's coming. If I ever…"

"Mom! Slow down and stop talking to yourself! People are staring!"

"That's your hat they're looking at, Annabelle. Not me."

We were practically jogging. "He's gone, Mom. Slow down, please!" We rounded a corner and Mom came to such a sudden stop that I ran into her. "Jeez!"

She took a deep breath and looked around. "I don't see him. Are you sure it was him?"

"Yes. But running all over Portland isn't going to do us any good, beyond strengthening our calf muscles." I grabbed her arm. "We'll tell the police, okay? Right now, let's get a cab...."

"A streetcar is coming. Let's catch that. It will take us toward Helmer's."

"Mom, I really don't want a new hat. I have lots of hats. I'll take this off if it really bothers you that much."

I reached up to pull off my sock monkey, but she stopped me, planting her palm on top of my head. "Don't move."

"What."

"I see him. Over there, in front of that coffee shop."

I turned around and sure enough, there was Scranton, leaning against a shop window. Mom started off in his direction, but I grabbed her again. "No, Mom. Stop."

"He doesn't get to stalk us, Annabelle."

"We don't know that he *is* stalking us. We need a plan before we go after him. I mean, a plan beyond you kicking him with your boots." I suddenly wished I had bought that gray suede pair that would last me a lifetime. "Why don't I call the police right now, tell them that he's here, and then...?" I stopped short, because in that moment, Loren Scranton stepped out in the street, where an oncoming car hurled him high in the air to land like a brick.

Without another thought we ran toward him, Mom telling me to call an ambulance.

Two emergency calls in two days. This vacation of mine was starting to feel as disastrous as the one Burt Reynolds took in *Deliverance*. At least I was in Portland and not canoeing down the rapids of the Cahulawassee River, hunted by inbreds.

Chapter Six

I called Mickey while Mom was administering aid to Scranton—who was unconscious on the street—and we waited for the ambulance.

"I'm going to get Mom out of here as soon as I can, Mickey."

"Babe. Wait and talk to the police. Tell them about Scranton and…"

"There are tons of witnesses here, including the driver. It wasn't a hit and run. We don't have to stay."

"Where's Sylvia?"

"Crouching next to Scranton and holding a cloth against his head. Someone gave it to her. A restaurant napkin, I think."

"She'll need to apprise the EMT of his condition…."

"She can tell someone else right now what she knows about his condition and turn the first aid over to that someone else. We need to get the hell out of here. What if Scranton is involved and he has some partner lurking…?"

"Who could follow you if you leave, but if you stay…"

"We'll get a cab."

"You're scared."

"You bet your bookie I am."

"I think you're safer if you wait for the police, with that crowd of people."

I shook my head, like he could see me. "Mickey, I was slipped a gun and Claudia whatshername got beat up. Scranton is maybe stalking me. He might be looking for the backpack. Who knows what the hell could happen next? I just want to get out of here." I could hear the ambulance siren several blocks away. "The EMTs are almost here."

"Okay. Go home. Call the police from there. Tell them your suspicions about Scranton. Be careful. Call me when you get home. Text me on the way."

I could see the ambulance now. "Okay. We're outta here."

"Text me," he repeated.

I hung up and kneeled down next to Mom. "We have to leave."

She looked at me, alarmed. "We can't until he is in the hands of…"

I motioned to a young man squatting next to Mom. "Will you please take over applying pressure on this wound? And if he wakes up, try to keep him still. It looks like his arm is broken." He nodded and moved into position, while I eased Mom away.

"Annabelle, this is wrong. We should stay…."

But she didn't finish her sentence. The look on my face, I can only assume, convinced her quickly that it was time for us to split.

We hustled over to the front of the Benson Hotel several blocks away, where the doorman hailed a cab for us. We were silent on the ride home and were there in fifteen minutes. I paid the driver while Mom scrambled out and up the stairs to the front door, fiddling for her key, then rushing in when Dad opened the door.

I walked in to hear Dad calling after Mom, who was running upstairs, "Syl? Something wrong?" Then he turned to me. "Bea?"

"I'm sorry, Dad." And then I started to cry, and he started to reach for me, but then changed his mind and dashed upstairs to see after Mom.

Dawson listened carefully while Mom and I detailed the afternoon's events. Monroe did his wandering-around-the-room-looking-at-everything routine, like we were harboring stolen artwork or hiding a secret door leading to a basement where we held girls in slavery. He stopped his meandering when Mom tried to explain why we left.

"We simply don't know what's going on, or how we're involved, you see, Detective Dawson, and Annabelle thought we should get to a safe place and then call you." She smiled brightly.

Monroe spoke up. "Against the law to leave the scene of an accident."

I stood up. "Give me a break. We weren't involved in the accident. We were helping until the ambulance got there."

"So you say."

We had a stare-down. "What does that mean?"

He shrugged. "Maybe you had something to do with Mr. Scranton getting hit by that car."

I guffawed. "Oh, right. Like, what, we pushed him? We already told you, we were across the street, kitty-corner to where he was. We watched him walk in front of that car."

"So you say."

Dawson coughed. "Look, we have some information about that gun."

"Let's hear it." Dad looked like he was about ready to throw Monroe out of the house.

"Well, unfortunately, it was used in a murder, here, in Portland, a couple of weeks ago. Ballistics matched the gun to bullets."

"Good!" I said. "Then you know whose gun it is!"

Dawson shook his head. "We tracked the serial number. The gun was reported stolen about a year ago. There's only one set of prints on it, which must be yours. It had been wiped clean otherwise."

Mom's bright smile had vanished. "Annabelle wasn't here two weeks ago," she practically snarled.

"No, ma'am, we know Annabelle didn't commit that murder." Dawson paused.

Monroe broke in. "But she could be connected, since she has the gun."

I snickered. "And that's why I called you and turned it over to you? Give me a break."

Dad patted my knee. "Detectives, what about Scranton? Is he okay, do you know?"

"He's got a broken arm and a concussion. He was lucky." Monroe was staring at me while he said this, and I didn't avert my eyes, which wasn't easy since he had an orange crumb or something stuck on his mustache and I kept looking at it.

"He doesn't need to know that Mom took care of him, right?"

"Right," answered Monroe. "But we'll ask him if he was following you."

"*Will* ask?" snipped Mom. "You mean, you haven't asked him already? The accident was four hours ago!"

Monroe broke our gaze to trade looks with Dawson.

Dad stood up. "Don't tell me, he's already left the hospital."

Dawson nodded. "Checked himself out as soon as the cast was on his arm and he saw an opportunity. But don't worry, folks, we'll find him."

"Oh, for fuck's sake," moaned Mom.

Dawson stood up to leave and motioned Monroe toward the door. "Stick around, Annabelle? You're in town for a week, I think?"

"Yes."

"Good."

Monroe reached for the front door handle, but I stopped him. "Monroe!"

He turned toward me.

"You've got Cheese Doodles stuck on your mustache."

He stared at me. I pointed at my own lip with my finger. "Right about here."

Right on cue, Dusty barked.

The cops left.

Chapter Seven

I was having a hard time sleeping, what with jetlag and stressing about a gun with my prints all over it. I was missing Mickey more than ever, especially since I had made tuna melts for my parents after the police left. I'm not much of a cook, but I make a mean TM. The secret is in the butter, but that's all I'm saying. Anyway, Mickey loves them and I cook them at home once a week, on Sundays.

Mom and Dad were appreciative, but not in the way Mickey usually is. If you get my drift.

I had called him earlier, to tell him about the gun being used in a murder and how I didn't like Monroe much. He promised to come out as soon as possible. I could hear the worry in his voice, so I tried to sound just fine and dandy on the phone. But I wasn't.

I texted him at eleven, two in the morning his time. "U missed TMs 2nite."

He responded, "I missed more than that. U OK?"

"OK. Lonely."

"Surprise 4 U tomorrow."

"U????!!!!!"

"No. But good surprise. Get some sleep."

"XXOO."

"Ditto."

I eventually did fall asleep, and woke up when I heard Dusty barking downstairs. Then the doorbell rang. And then it rang again.

I squinted at the clock—it was ten already. I figured Mom and Dad must have gone out. So I threw the afghan over my shoulders and went downstairs.

Whoever was at the door was insistent. He or she pushed the buzzer twice more in as much time as it took me to get there. It made me a little nervous, so I yelled, "Hold your pants on, I'm coming!" and peeked through the front window to see who was there.

Then I threw open the door.

"*Hola, amiga!*"

I threw my arms around Luis while Dusty bounced around us. "You're my surprise! Oh, Luis, it is so good to see you! Come in!"

Like I already said, Mickey and I met Luis in Las Vegas when we got ourselves in a heap of trouble, and he helped us out even when we were strangers to him. He's now our best friend in the world. I think of him as the kindest, most generous friend anyone could ever imagine—maybe he's the Latino version of Paul Newman in *Butch Cassidy and the Sundance Kid*, if Robert Redford was Mickey, and I was Katharine Ross, the girlfriend. Except that we're not outlaws and I don't think Luis could balance me on the handlebars of his bike while "Raindrops Keep Falling on my Head" plays in the background. But he'd try if I asked him to.

Luis dropped his bag on the floor and gave Dusty a hearty pet before he gave me a second hug. "I am here to help, however I can."

"Let's have some coffee."

We settled at the dining room table with our mugs, toast, and jam. Luis told me that Mickey booked his flight from Las Vegas last night. "He is worried about you, Annabelle. He is upset that he is not here himself. But it is important to find that boy."

"I know, Luis. And don't take this the wrong way, but you're the next best thing." I smiled. "And really, I don't know what there is to be done."

"Any word on the man who you met at the airport?"

"Loren Scranton. No. He left the hospital and the police haven't found him."

"And the girl?"

"Claudia. Still in a coma. Her parents are arriving in Portland today, according to the police."

Luis sipped his coffee. "They took their time getting here, *sí?* Claudia was attacked on Monday and now it is Wednesday. What about this murder? Do you have any details?"

I sat up straight. "Just heard about that last night. But, yup, maybe we can find out more about it. They said it happened a couple of weeks ago."

"That is a start." He paused. "Did they return your backpack to you?"

I shook my head. "No. Because it was found at the crime scene, they're keeping it until they figure this whole thing out." I slathered more jam on my toast. "Is it me?"

"Is what you, *amiga?*"

"Is there something about me that gets me into these impossible situations?"

Luis chuckled. "You stand out in a crowd, this is true. And I know that I am happy that your previous misfortune brought us together. But, no, *amiga*, you only have *mala suerte*."

"What is that?"

"Bad luck."

I raised my eyebrows. *"Mucho mala suerte."*

Luis reached his hand out to me across the table. "We will figure this out."

I grabbed it. "You are *el mejor*."

He laughed. *"Qué bueno."*

Just then the back door opened and Mom and Dad walked in, flushed and tittering. "Why, hello!" Mom brushed her thick gray hair from her face as she focused on Luis.

Luis stood up and held out his hand. "It is my pleasure to meet you. I am Luis Maldonado."

Mom considered his hand and then hugged him. "Holy shit, Luis, I'm so glad to meet you at last!"

When she let him go, he shook hands with Dad, and I beamed, feeling blessed, lucky, and safe. "Mickey flew him in."

Dad nodded. "Good man, Mick. And you, too, Luis. Thanks for making the trip."

"It is my pleasure, Mr. Starkey."

"Jeff. And this is Sylvia." He motioned to me. "Pajamas, Bea?"

I pulled the blanket tighter around me. "I slept late. I'll go change, and then maybe we can all figure out what our plan is for the day."

Mom plopped herself down on the couch. "I know exactly what we're going to do today. We're going to visit that poor girl in the hospital."

I was halfway up the stairs. "She's in a coma, Mom. Won't do much good." I kept walking.

"There might be a clue in her room."

I stopped, turned, and scooted back down. "What are you talking about?"

"Yes, darling," added Dad. "Do tell." Luis sat down and studied Mom.

"Well, just a little detective work. Nothing wrong with seeing if she has anything in her pockets, or if her chart gives us any information we don't already have, or we could find out if she's had any visitors, or…"

"Mom! We're not detectives!"

She rolled her eyes. "You almost are, and Luis is here now, so…"

Dad interrupted her. "I'm not sure this is a good idea."

"It's NOT!" I stood in front of my parents. "We do not want to piss off the police and…"

This time Luis interrupted me. "Actually, *amiga*, Sylvia's idea is not a bad one. A quick visit. If anyone is suspicious, we can say that we are concerned, that is all."

Mom jumped up. "I knew I'd like you, Luis."

I groaned. "I'm getting dressed. But maybe just Luis and I should go to the hospital. All four of us? That's a little much." I turned to face Luis so Mom and Dad couldn't see me and made a face that I hoped said, *Right? You're going to agree with me, right?*

"I think that would be a wise move," offered Luis, as he winked at me.

Mom sat back down. "Crap. I just want to help."

Dad grinned. "You have, darling, by making the plan for the day. Now, Bea, get dressed, we'll all get some breakfast or lunch or whatever we're eating at eleven o'clock in the morning, and then you and Luis can get going."

I started back up the stairs, then stopped again, and called down. "Where were you guys this morning, anyway?"

Silence.

So down the stairs I went again. Mom and Dad were making faces at each other like some special sign language. "Hello? Did you hear me?"

Dad walked over to me and put his arm around me. "You don't get to know everything, except that no harm was done to us or by us this morning and all is well. Now, really, Bea, will you please get dressed?" He kissed the side of my head.

I frowned at Mom, who gave me a fake, toothy smile. "Darling, those pajamas really are not becoming."

I exhaled loudly and trudged back upstairs.

What the hell was going on with them?

Chapter Eight

The hospital where Claudia Bigelow lay in a coma is a teaching hospital, perched on a hill high above the city. I drove Luis and myself up the winding drive with Dad's words in my head about driving carefully and obeying the speed limit. I pride myself on my excellent driving record (just one ticket, and it really wasn't fair: I glided through that one red light, fully aware that no traffic was coming), so I didn't know what he was going on about, except that he might have been expecting me to land myself in yet another mishap. The truth was, I hadn't driven in a while, since I don't need a car in Manhattan, and the Mazda 3 was pretty sporty and fun to drive. So, yeah, I was speeding a bit. Just a bit.

Then I saw the police car lights blinking behind me.

"Oh, no. This is ridiculous." I pulled to the side while Luis turned around to look out the back window.

"Be calm, Annabelle. Sweet. Lots of smiles." He gave me a big one, just as fake as my mother's earlier.

I rolled down the window. "Hello, Officer."

"License and registration, please."

I dug my license out of my purse. Luis routed around the glove compartment for the registration. We produced both.

"You were going thirty. This is a tricky road with all the turns."

"Sorry. We're anxious to go see our friend in the hospital. She's in a coma." I pretended to wipe a tear from my cheek.

"New York?"

I nodded. "Manhattan. Visiting my parents here in Portland."

He stared at me, like he was waiting for a better explanation.

"Great city you've got here. Not as big as my city, of course, but it has a lot going for it. Like the river. Well, Manhattan has rivers, too, of course. But Portland has, well, really great food trucks and I think the airport is super duper." I flashed my pearly whites.

The policeman handed the documents back to me. "Watch yourself, Ms. Starkey. This isn't New York. We take things a little easier here."

"Roger that, sir. Ten four."

Then the cop peeked in at Luis. "Are you visiting, too?"

I felt Luis tense up. I did, too. Why question my passenger?

"Yes." Luis held the cop's eyes for what felt like a full minute.

I broke the spell. "Thank you, again, um, Officer...?" I squinted at the name on his jacket. "Officer Foley?" I laughed. "Is your first name Axel?"

He frowned. "No."

"You know, Eddie Murphy? *Beverly Hills Cop*? C'mon, you must have seen it." Big smile.

He paused. "Hope your friend is okay. Have a nice day." Then he walked back to his patrol car.

I turned to Luis. "What the hell, Luis? Why was he so curious about you?"

"*Amiga,* I am brown." He was jotting something down on a business card he had taken out of his wallet.

I shook my head. "I don't want to believe that. Damn. I wonder if he was following us. I wonder if the Portland PD is keeping a close eye on little ole me." I leaned over to look at his note. "What are you writing?"

"Foley's name and badge number. Just in case." He stuck the card back in his wallet. "Now, *por favor, mas despacio.*"

"Dispatch with all due haste?"

Luis peered at me over his sunglasses. "More slowly, *amiga.*"

We continued on our way to visit Claudia.

◇◇◇

Claudia was not in the ICU, so it was easy to visit her—especially since there were no police officers posted by her room. Luis told me that wasn't unusual. It was difficult to commit manpower to guarding victims except in high-profile cases.

Claudia's room had two beds in it, but she was the only patient. I was glad to see that she wasn't on a ventilator and was breathing on her own. Her face was swollen and bruised, but otherwise she looked like a normal sleeping person.

"She is young, yes?" asked Luis.

"Twenty, according to her Facebook page." I went to the closet. "Nothing here, except her clothes."

Luis opened the drawer in the bedside table. "A pair of glasses, broken." He pulled it out further. "Ah. What is this?" He plucked a tissue out of a box and used it to pick up a piece of paper. "A note. 'You are going to die if you don't listen to me.'" He held it out to me. "It is crumpled. Like it was in her pocket."

I took it and read it myself. "The handwriting is very neat. Not scribbled in haste. Like the person who wrote it is calm and sane, but I'm thinking this person is probably neither."

I put it on the wheelie overbed table and took a picture of it with my phone. Luis returned it to the drawer. "She was in trouble, this Claudia."

"Yes. Maybe a bad boyfriend." I walked to the side of the bed and took Claudia's hand in mine. "You hang in there, Claudia. I don't know how you're connected to that gun, but Luis and I, we're going to try to make sure you don't have to use it. Ever." I squeezed her hand, and then we left.

We were quiet driving home, but after I entered my parents' driveway, I turned off the ignition and sat back. "Let's have some drinks downtown tonight."

"This will help, you think?"

"Let's have them with Nancy and Phillip Bigelow. We'll call the hotels and find out where they're staying."

"*Bueno.* And let's find out about that murder."

We both got out of the car. "Mom and Dad can help."

He raised his eyebrows at me. "You would like this?"

I smiled. "Actually, yes. As long as Mom behaves and doesn't swear at the Bigelows too much."

Luis laughed. "She is a pistol, your mother. I like her very much."

"So far, you do, Luis. So far."

We went inside.

Chapter Nine

It didn't take me long to find out that the Bigelows were staying at The Nines, discovered with only my third phone call to downtown hotels. The receptionist connected me, and Nancy Bigelow answered. "Hello?"

"Mrs. Bigelow?"

"Who is this?"

"Annabelle Starkey. I met your daughter, sort of. My parents and I found her shortly after she was attacked, at the Japanese Garden. I was…"

"Aaah. Yes. The police told me. She had your backpack."

"Yes." I heard her sigh. "I'm so sorry about your daughter. I would like to help if I can."

"The police are taking care of things."

"I'm sure they're doing a great job. But I'm employed by a detective agency in New York, and one of my partners is here, and we'd like to buy you and your husband a drink and learn some more about Claudia, what she was doing in Portland, and…"

"My husband?"

"Phillip."

She snorted. "Yes, Ms. Starkey, I know his name. How did you?"

I paused. I didn't want to let on that we had been investigating the Bigelows on Facebook, but…"We looked you up, online."

Another sigh. "You did. Hmm. Well, Phillip isn't here yet. I expect he'll arrive around six. He was out of town on business and is flying in."

"How about the hotel bar, seven o'clock?"

She made a little clucking sound. "I suppose that would be fine. See you then."

"Right. Thanks. Good-bye." We hung up.

Mom, Dad, and Luis were sitting around the dining room table listening to my side of the conversation, and when I put the phone down, I answered their inquiring looks. "Seven. We're on."

"Great!" Mom slapped the table and stood up. "What shall we do until then? It's only four."

"The murder. Research. And before either of you jump in," I said, regarding Mom and Dad, "Luis and I will take care of this, along with Mickey. You two do whatever you do at four o'clock in the afternoon." I flashed a big smile.

Dad rose and stretched. "Nap for me." He kissed Mom's cheek and patted my shoulder as he left the room.

Mom looked a bit at loose ends. "Well, if you really don't need my help, I'll pay some bills and send a few e-mails." She waited, hoping, I thought, that we would change our minds.

It was Luis' turn to stand. "*Señora* Sylvia, if you don't mind, I would very much like to take you up on your offer to help, with another little problem." Mom's eyes lit up as Luis continued. "Ruby, my wife, is pregnant, and…"

I flew out of my chair. "WHAT?! RUBY'S PREGNANT?"

Luis laughed. "*Sí, amiga.*"

I threw my arms around him. "Why didn't you say something right away?"

He hugged me. "I was under strict instructions not to say anything because she is still in the first trimester. But I could not help myself."

Mom chuckled. "Wonderful news, Luis. How can I help?"

Luis disentangled himself from me. "Sylvia, Ruby is concerned about the move to New York and starting with a new doctor. Can you help her figure out the best way to find the right doctor? Her clinic in Las Vegas does not have a recommendation."

Mom clapped her hands together. "You bet. Shall I give her a call?"

Luis nodded. "Just as soon as I call her, and let her know that the secret is no longer a secret. Thank you, Sylvia. Ruby has no mother anymore, and she is a little scared."

"Well, shit, of course she is." Mom beamed. Suddenly I realized how much she would enjoy a grandchild. How had I not known this before? I was immediately overcome both with gratitude that she hadn't pressured me about this, ever, and with guilt, knowing that I simply did not want to have a baby, ever.

I sat back down while Luis gave Mom Ruby's phone number and then slipped outside to call her. Mom, still beaming, walked around behind my chair and kissed the top of my head. "Lovely man, darling. He'll be a great father, I think." Then she scooted upstairs.

Left alone temporarily, I rubbed Dusty's ears and decided to take her for a quick walk. I leashed her and we ducked out the front door. It looked like it was about to rain, so I had put on my mother's heavy-duty rain jacket, with hood. We walked a few blocks west to a park, where I let Dusty off the leash so she could nose around in the bushes. No one else was there. I found a bench and sat down.

Babies. Mickey and I had talked about getting married, no serious conversation, just casual asides. But not about babies. What if he wanted one? What if he wanted several, like five or six? How was it possible that I hadn't considered this before, that Mickey might not feel the same way I did about having little ones?

I was happy, supremely happy, for Luis and Ruby. But when Mickey heard the news, would he start seeing me as mother material?

I couldn't be. I mean, I don't think I would be a Joan Crawford *Mommie-Dearest* clone, cruel and sadistic. But I couldn't see myself as Kate Winslet in *Finding Neverland* where she was raising all of those boys while coughing her head off and never issuing a cross word. Okay, I know there's a middle ground. But the long and short of it was this: I had no biological clock ticking. No yen for children. No mother instinct.

I'd have to talk to Mickey about this, probably soon.

I whistled for Dusty and attached her leash. The rain was just starting to fall as we reached home.

The murder committed with the backpack gun—Luis, Mickey, and I figured, after the three of us had done some research online—was of a young man of twenty-five. He was shot in the back, on a rainy night, in eastern Portland, near the Gresham border. He had come out of a bar, turned a corner onto a narrow side street, and had been unceremoniously gunned down. Two bullets: one to the back and another—administered after he was on the ground—to the back of his head.

Executed, in other words.

The murder was the only one we could find that happened in the two-week time frame. The victim's name was Hank Howard. He was an auto mechanic. By all reports, he was a normal kind of guy. No record, quiet, friends who loved him, solid family, parents married for thirty years. There were no suspects—at least that's what the news reports said.

We further researched Howard, looking for any connections to Seattle or the Bigelows, and came up with nothing. Luis suggested that we visit the bar where Howard was last seen, and Mickey, on speakerphone, thought that was a good idea. "But you shouldn't go, Anabelle."

"And why not?" I sputtered. "I'm the one most involved here, and just because I'm a girl without a gun doesn't mean that I can't pull my weight on my wagon, thank you very much." Metaphors come easily to me.

"Will you please calm down? I know you can pull your wagon, or whatever you just said. But if the police find out that you were asking questions in that bar, they'll be all over your ass again. If Luis goes by himself, they won't make the connection."

I groaned. "Unless Alex Foley is following us around."

"Huh? Eddie Murphy? What?"

Luis was remaining silent through this banter, but he chuckled at that. "The officer who pulled us over, Mick. When Annabelle was speeding."

"I WASN'T SPEEDING!"

Luis shrugged. Mickey said nothing.

"Well, okay, if you want to call that 'speeding.' But I wasn't putting anyone in danger."

"Babe, please, let Luis do this on his own. You can drive him there and stay in the car."

Luis leaned across the table toward me. "He is right, *amiga*."

I exhaled loudly. "I can't promise. I'll have to depend on how things feel when we're there." I paused. Mickey and Luis said nothing. "Look, I have to trust my instincts, just like you."

Mickey took a moment before he answered. "Our instincts don't seem to be in alignment. But you be damn careful."

"I will. But right now we should get going. We're off to meet the Bigelows."

"Okay. Call me later?"

"Yup."

"Annabelle, don't be pissed. I'm just…"

"I know, Mickey. It's weird not having you here. Lots going on, and the parents are weird, and Luis is, well, not weird, he's great, but I don't like any of this. And I don't like being told what I can't do."

"Luis, my friend, please tell Ruby how happy I am for you. Such great news. Outstanding news!"

Luis got up. "I will speak with you later, Mick." He left to give us some private time. I picked up the phone, taking it off speaker.

Mickey said, "Hey."

"Hey."

"I'll be there. One day, maybe two. I'm close to finding the boy."

"That's great."

"I hope so. Look, I don't like being away from you. You know that, right?"

"Yup. I do. It's just today, for some reason, I feel so unsettled." I did know the reason, and it was the baby news coupled with Mickey trying to save a child.

"Maybe that drink with the Bigelows will help. Hey, we got good news today, though, right? So exciting about Ruby being pregnant!"

"Absolutely! Yes!" *Uh oh,* I thought. *You wanna be a daddy.* I took a deep breath. "Mickey, we're together, no matter what, right? Like right and left guards?"

"Babe, what's this about? Yes, of course, no matter what. Are you okay, really?"

I nodded, even though he couldn't see me. "I want to kiss you."

"I want to do more than that."

"Is it getting hot in New York, because it's suddenly really warm in Portland."

He laughed. "I am stroking you in all the right places, right now, in my wide-awake dreams. And while I'm staking out a possible crime scene tonight, I will have a very hard time thinking of anything but you."

"Don't forget my flannel pajamas."

"Oh, I've already removed them."

"Be careful. And get your ass out here, along with the rest of you."

"Count on it."

We hung up.

Chapter Ten

The Nines Hotel is in the heart of downtown Portland. The lobby is on the eighth floor, where there are several casually delineated seating areas. Luis, Mom, Dad, and I scoured the busy lounge, looking for the Bigelows. Dad and I had seen Nancy's picture on Facebook, which ended up being a very good thing: there were dozens of couples enjoying the hip ambiance. Dad saw her first, and we made our way over.

"Mr. and Mrs. Bigelow?" I held out my hand. "Annabelle Starkey. This is my partner, Luis Maldonado, and these are my parents, Jeff and Sylvia Starkey."

Nancy and Phillip Bigelow both stood up and shook hands all around. After we sat and placed our cocktail orders with the waiter, Phillip drained his existing martini and popped the olive on the toothpick into his mouth. Chewing, he leaned back against the couch, his hands behind his head, and winked at me.

This, I thought, was as inappropriate as Kevin Spacey's father character in *American Beauty*, who lusts after his teenage daughter's friend. Okay, I'm not a teenager, and if Bigelow had an ounce of Spacey's class, maybe I wouldn't have been so disgusted by him. But he didn't, and I was.

Then he spoke. "So, you're a detective. You look more like a school teacher."

And you, I thought, *look like a basset hound, jowls and ears competing with each other for best in class.*

Dad reached over and put his hand on my arm before I could respond. "Annabelle's in a partnership with two detectives, based in New York. Lots of experience among them. What sort of work are you in, Phillip?" He squeezed my arm and let go, his eyes not leaving the basset's.

"Does it matter? Aren't we here to talk about Claudia? What do you all know so far?"

Nancy Bigelow was keeping quiet. Her gin and tonic was drained, and she was looking around nervously, like the next one couldn't come a moment too soon.

Mom, not one to hold her tongue, didn't hold it this time, either. "Well, well, Phillip, and Nancy, we're very concerned about your daughter as well as ours. She has become involved in this crap without having done anything to deserve it. She was going to try to help your daughter, and all that's happened to Annabelle so far is the police have been interrogating her like she's some sort of fucking criminal, and you seem to think it's okay to treat her like a little girl."

Mom started looking around for a drink to appear, too.

Phillip laughed. "Okay. Sorry. Wrong foot. I'm beat from the trip, and all of this has got me off my game." He winked at me again.

I squinted at him. "You know what I say…"

He leaned toward me. "What's that, Anna?"

"Annabelle. I say, 'If you wink, better not blink.'" I had just made that up, but I stared at him with what I hoped was a glare that would put Linda Hamilton's Sarah Connor from *The Terminator II* to shame.

Mom guffawed. "That's a good one, honey."

Phillip looked confused, Nancy was now tossing nuts down her throat like she hadn't eaten in a year, and Dad rubbed his face.

Luis—perhaps wishing he was home with his pregnant wife and not surrounded by the hotheaded Starkey women—stepped up. "Mr. and Mrs. Bigelow, we are all very upset about the circumstances. We appreciate you meeting us for a drink. We wonder if you have any ideas about who could have attacked

Claudia, and if you know why she was expecting to pick up a backpack with a gun at the airport."

The waiter showed up then, and distributed our cocktails. I sipped my bourbon, Mom quickly downed a gulp of chardonnay, Dad swallowed some Scotch, and Nancy and Phillip both drank from their glasses like alcohol was nectar from the gods. Luis was reaching for his beer glass when Nancy spoke up.

"It's that boyfriend. He's been trouble all along."

Phillip nodded. "We told the police. On the phone. But they say they checked him out, and they can't confirm that he was even in town when all this happened."

"What is his name?" Luis asked.

"Wes something, right Nance?"

"Wesley Young. He and Claudia have been dating off and on for about six months."

"And you don't like him?" asked Dad.

"He hit her once," Nancy responded, then drank some more.

I was watching Phillip through this conversation, and he winced when Nancy said that. It was like the memory pained him as much as the first time he heard it. So I considered that maybe he wasn't such a horrible man. Maybe he really loved his daughter and was just upset.

"That's horrible!" said Mom. "Did she press charges?"

Nancy shook her head. "Wouldn't do it. I tried to get her to talk to the police, but she refused. This was about a month ago, now."

Phillip stood up. "He's the only dirtbag we can think of, who would have done this. Sorry, I have to take a piss." He wandered off.

Nancy seemed to relax a bit immediately upon Phillip's departure. "I visited her today. She looks terrible. I spoke loudly to her, they told me to do that, but she didn't respond at all. I don't know what to do..." She trailed off while she pulled a tissue out of her purse and dabbed her eyes.

Mom moved over and sat next to her on the couch. She put her arm around her. "All you can do is continue to visit her and tell her you love her."

I jumped in. "Mom's a doctor. Look, Mrs. Bigelow, do you think Claudia was getting the gun for herself, or for someone else? She said to me on the phone that she needed a detective. It sounded like she was in a lot of trouble…well, I mean, obviously she was, since she was attacked and all." It was my turn to take a drink.

"I don't know. I don't think she's ever shot a gun."

"No guns in your house?" asked Luis.

Nancy hesitated. "Phillip has one, but he keeps it in our bedroom, and Claudia has never touched it, as far as I know. She told us that guns scare her. That's why this isn't making any sense. You know, she's not well. She's had some emotional troubles. Perhaps they're normal for a girl her age. Perhaps it's because she was adopted…"

At that, Nancy started crying, full force, into Mom's shoulder. Dad and I looked at each other and wordlessly agreed to cut this short and leave these people alone. Dad signaled the waiter for the bill.

But Luis had one more question. "I am sorry to pester you, but can you tell us one more thing, please? Have you ever heard of Hank Howard or Loren Scranton?"

Nancy collected herself. "No. The police asked me that, too, earlier today. Who are they?"

"They might be related to your daughter's case, and might not be." Luis smiled. "Thank you for talking with us."

Phillip came back as we were standing to leave. "Are you going to let us know what you find out?"

"Sure," I said. "Give me your cell phone number."

"I'd love to," he winked again, "but damn it, I left it in Miami. Better just call Nancy at the hotel. She doesn't use her cell much, do you Nance?"

Nancy ignored him but wrote her cell number on a bar napkin anyway.

Luis was shifting his jaw back and forth, which is something he does when he's uptight. "That will be a big inconvenience for you, I would think with your business? No cell phone?"

"I can reach out when I need to. I'll be back in Miami in a couple of days, anyway."

Wow, I thought. *With your kid in a coma. What an asshole.*

"What did you say you do for a living?" asked Dad.

"Didn't say, old man, but since you're all so interested, I'm in ball bearings."

There didn't seem to be an appropriate response to this news, so we all smiled politely, thanked them again, and got on the elevator back down to street level.

"Ball bearings?" Mom practically shouted. "Is that some kind of male stripper act?"

I howled. "Hey, you know, that might have been a better line in *The Graduate,* instead of 'plastics.'"

Luis frowned, and I realized he had never seen the movie. I'd have to fix that.

Chapter Eleven

The four of us had dinner in the bar area of the Veritable Quandary, and according to Dad, we lucked out finding an available table. The popular restaurant is near the Willamette River, which runs north/south through the city, and it's cozy, old-fashioned, and trendy all at the same time. The long, wooden bar sits opposite a row of high-backed wooden booths, and the backdrop of liquor bottles reaches up to the ceiling. The brick walls are complemented by dark wood shelving and large arch-topped windows facing the street.

I asked our waiter to take a picture of us, which I then texted to Mickey.

He wrote back,

> Say hi to all. And pick up the tab. Call me when you get back to the house. No matter what time. Have to talk. XO.

I showed this to Luis, who frowned. "Do you think something is wrong, *amiga*?"

I put the phone back in my purse. "Wrong, or important." I raised my glass to Luis and Mom and Dad. "Thanks, all of you. This meal is on me and Mickey." We clinked and said "cheers" all around, and then dug into our meals.

Back at the house, Mom set up the futon in the den for Luis' bed, and I settled in under the duvet upstairs and called Mickey.

"Hey," he answered.

"Hey, yourself. What's up? It's one-thirty in New York–land. Did you find the boy?"

I could hear him yawn. "That apartment I was watching was a dead end, but I've got another idea."

"You need to sleep."

"Need to talk to you. This guy that got murdered, Hank Howard?"

"Yup."

"He wasn't such a sweet young man, as it turns out. I found out that he moved to Portland just a few months ago from New York. He was a druggie, owed his supplier a lot of money, and split town because he couldn't pay up."

I sat up in bed. "How in the world did you find that out?"

He yawned again. "I was having a beer with Kermit, you know, my ex-partner—he just got promoted, by the way, to Sergeant—and told him the situation you're in. I mentioned Howard's name, and he knew all about him."

"Weird."

"Very. Turns out his real name is Howard Hanks. He switched it around in Portland. Not very creative, alias-wise. The Portland police probably have figured out who Howard or Hanks is, er, was, and they probably see this as another connection to you, since…"

"Since I just flew in from New York."

"Bingo."

"Crap."

"Right. So, maybe going to the bar tomorrow is not such a good idea. It will just tie you in further with this mess."

"I still think Luis and I should go. Finding out who killed him could help us figure out where the gun came from and how Claudia is involved."

Mickey sighed. "It's too dangerous, babe. Even with Luis there, you shouldn't go anywhere near that bar."

I clenched my teeth. Mickey loves me, of course, and he wants to protect me, and mostly, I love that. But I have deeply ingrained resistance to anyone telling me what I should or shouldn't do. It started when I was a kid, in the third grade. My teacher, Miss Klipple—who I figured was about ninety years old—told me that I *should* be nicer to Tommy Madison, even though he told me at every opportunity that I threw like a girl and ran like a turtle. I probably shouldn't have tackled him during the recess softball game when he was about to tag me out at second base, but hell, he only got a scrape on the back of his head that needed a measly seven stitches. The point is, he never spoke to me again after that. Mission accomplished.

I had a few boyfriends, too, in high school and college, who loved to correct my English, or expound on all the things I *should* know more about. Bruckner's symphonies, the geological strata of the Grand Canyon, the benefits and drawbacks of root vegetables, and why daylight-saving time should be abolished are monologues I recall, from four different guys, mind you. What I don't recall is ever showing the least bit of interest in any of those topics.

So I took a breath and reminded myself that this was Mickey talking, not any of those jerks, and that Miss Klipple had probably been looking out for my best interests. "Hon. I know you worry about me. But I'll be fine."

Mickey didn't respond.

"Hon?"

"Yeah, still here. Wishing I was there. Luis and I should be working on this together, while you should be enjoying visiting the 'rents."

"All three of us should be working on this together, and we are. I'm part of the detective agency, remember?"

He didn't answer right away, and then said, "Call me after you and Luis leave the bar?"

"Definitely. Mickey, something's weird with Mom and Dad. They were out this morning and were all squirrely about it when they got back. Didn't want to say what they were doing."

Mickey laughed. "Maybe they went somewhere to have some hot sex!"

"Ew! Mickey! Don't talk about my parents having hot sex! Ew!"

"They're great people, Annabelle. You're lucky to have them. They'll let you know if something important is going on."

"You're right. I know." I snuggled back underneath the covers. "Are you coming out here?"

"I'll know more tomorrow. Hang in there."

"How's Bonkers?"

"Driving me crazy. He perches on top of my chest when I get in bed and head-butts me."

I giggled. "He's starting to love you, sweetie."

"I think I liked it better when he growled at me and hid under the bed."

"Go to sleep now. I love you."

"I count on that, every minute of every day."

I hung up, set the phone on the bedside table, and quickly fell asleep.

Chapter Twelve

The name of the bar where Howard Hanks was last seen is called The Rowdy Yeats, which cracked me up. Whoever came up with that showed some real class, in my opinion.

I parked the car and got out right after Luis, punched the lock button, and started to head across the street to the front door until Luis stopped me, holding my arm gently. "Annabelle, I still think you should wait in the car."

"Luis, the name of this bar—I'm going to like the owner. The owner is going to like me. I'll get more information than you will."

"I do not understand."

"Rowdy Yates was Clint Eastwood's character on 'Rawhide,' an old TV show—it was Eastwood's break-out role—but it was spelled differently. Y-e-a-t-s, on the other hand…"

"Yes, I know. The poet."

"Right you are. So, I'm going in."

"Mickey was clear…"

"Mickey and you and I are partners. He's not in charge. Let's go." I patted Luis on the shoulder and we proceeded into the bar.

The Rowdy Yeats looked like a dump from the outside, but inside, it was pretty cool, for a dark bar where three rusty-looking men sat at noon, empty shot glasses and half-empty draft beers in front of them, staring at a soccer game on the wide-screen TV. It was clean—I could tell, even in the half-light, that the tables were wiped and the floor wasn't sticky—and there were photographs on the walls of, you guessed it, Eastwood and Yeats. Dark green ruffled curtains framed the windows, and a tiffany-style lamp hung from the ceiling over the pool table at the back.

Luis and I sat on a couple of stools. The bartender made his way to us and patted his hand on the bar. "What'll it be, kids?"

I smiled. He wasn't old enough to call us "kids." I figured him around forty-five, tops. "Beer for me, Pops. What do you have?"

He smiled. "Stella, Blue Moon, and Guinness."

"No brainer there. It's gotta be Guinness, surrounded as we are by Mr. Yeats."

"Same for me, please," said Luis.

He patted the bar top again and withdrew to fill our glasses. The three guys at the bar turned around to size us up, smiled, nodded, and went back to their soccer game.

"Luis, I don't get soccer. I think it's boring. Is it boring for you?"

Luis was watching the television. "Boring, *amiga*? You have much to learn about soccer! I was the goalie for my high-school team. I was good, too." He turned back to me. "My kid, he, she, whatever, my kid is going to play soccer. All children play soccer now. You might have to learn it, *amiga*, so that you can play with my son or daughter." Big smile.

I tried to mirror the big smile but said only, "I'll take your child to the movies instead."

Our beers showed up, and we each had a swallow, setting them back down on the bar. "Yum," I said, to the bartender. "Thanks. What's your name?"

"Perry. Haven't seen you two in here before."

"No," answered Luis, "this is our first time. It is a nice place you have."

"Thanks. I put a lot into it."

"You're the owner?" I asked.

Perry nodded. "Bought it five years ago and fixed it up. The neighborhood is up and coming. Got a good mix of old-timers and younger people who are moving in."

I held out my hand. "May I congratulate you on a brilliant name?"

He shook it. "Thanks." He laughed. "Most people don't get it. I know it's an odd name for a bar, but I think it's memorable. On Tuesday nights I play old 'Rawhide' episodes, and on Wednesday nights, we have poetry readings."

"Brilliant. Sounds very Portland to me."

Luis and I chatted with Perry, telling him that we were visiting from out of town, and asking him for suggestions of things to do in Portland. He was friendly and cheerful, jotted down the names of some restaurants and bars he recommended on a bar napkin, and then excused himself to tend to another customer who came in.

Luis said, "It is time to ask him about Hank Howard, yes?"

"Yes." I sipped my beer. "I like this place. It seems safe and fun and neighborly. Not a place for drug dealers."

"I agree."

Perry headed back our way in a few minutes. "Anything else I can get for you two?"

"Actually, *amigo*, we have a question for you."

"Shoot."

"The man who was shot and killed nearby recently. He was in here?"

Perry backed away from us and stiffened. "Who are you?"

Luis and I both pulled out our Asta Investigations business cards and handed them over to Perry. "PIs?" he read. "DDS? You're a dentist for a P.I. firm? What the hell?" He tossed the cards aside.

"Luis is a detective. I work for the agency as a partner. It's just starting up in New York. I'm not a dentist. I, um, dumpster dive, as needed."

He stared at me like I was a lunatic, then shifted over to Luis. "Why are you asking about Hank? Why are you investigating this?"

"We only want to know if maybe there are friends of his that come here, that we could talk to. We don't want to get anyone in trouble. We just need to find out some information."

Perry shook his head. "Some information? The police are all over this thing. Why don't you talk to them?"

"Perry." I reached out my hand across the bar as though I was going to hold his, but of course, that wasn't going to happen, so I pulled it back. "The gun used in the murder. Someone planted it on me, probably by mistake, and we're trying to figure out who did that and why."

Perry folded his arms across his chest and frowned. "Should I be calling the police right now, telling them that you're here and that you're connected to the gun?"

I shook my head. "No, they already know about me. Really. Look, can you just tell us one thing?" He recrossed his arms and didn't say anything, so I kept talking. "Do you know either Loren Scranton or Wesley Young?"

"No."

"Did you know that Hank Howard was a drug addict from New York?" Luis asked.

Perry's eyes got wide as he leaned toward Luis, his forearms on the bar. "We don't have drugs in this bar. No dealers, no smokers, none of that. Hank came in here for beers and companionship. He was a nice guy. I never had any trouble from him, and I never heard anyone saying a bad word about him." He stood up. "I won't have people talking about this place like it's a hangout for criminals."

"What did Hank tell you about himself, then?"

Perry turned to me. "He was quiet. And I don't pry."

"Did he have any hobbies, or a girlfriend, or did he have a job, or…?"

"Look!" Perry was leaning toward me, now. "I told you, his life was none of my business. If people don't want to talk, I don't press it."

I nodded. "I'm sorry. We don't mean to piss you off. It is just very upsetting to find my backpack was switched at the airport with one holding the gun that shot Hank. Actually, his name was Howard Hanks. Anyway, I appreciate your help, and I really do love your bar, and you've been very nice to us. I'm sorry, again."

Perry's shoulders relaxed a little bit. He picked up our glasses and put them in the sink. "You know, I just this minute remembered something. Hank, or Howard, or whatever his name was, he liked a girl. He told me he was really happy about it. He didn't tell me her name. He said she liked to play pool and that he would meet up with her at the Uptown Billiards Club. This was probably a week before he got shot."

Luis placed a twenty on the bar. "Thank you, Perry, for your help. We are grateful. And we are very pleased to meet you and spend time in your establishment."

I grabbed my purse and stood up, too. "Ditto, all of that, Perry. Maybe we'll come back for 'Rawhide' night or poetry."

Perry sighed. "Don't bring any trouble with you, that's all I ask."

◇◇◇

Luis was on the phone with Mickey as soon as I pulled away from the curb. "Mick, yes, she went in with me. It was fine. The bartender was helpful. We have another lead." And then he told him about the Uptown Billiards Club.

I was forgetting about being afraid and in danger and instead imagining this billiards club and what I might wear when we all went there later that night, figuring that, of course, we would. Ask some questions, see if we could find out about Howard Hanks' girl, maybe she was Claudia.

I love to play pool! I'm pretty good, but more important, how can you not feel hot, playing pool? Leaning over the table, shifting your hip to the side as you line up a shot, hearing the smashing of those balls. It's enough to make a nonsmoker like me want a cigarette, just thinking about it.

Luis hung up. "Mickey, he is relieved that our meeting with Perry went well, but he is on edge. He wants to talk to you later."

I bit my lip, sorry that I had worried Mickey, but feeling good about the progress Luis and I were making. "Is his case finished?"

"He sounds optimistic. Like he is getting close, maybe tonight."

"Luis, look, do you still want to move to New York? I mean, you and Ruby? Since the baby is coming and all?"

"Yes, *amiga,* we are decided. Ruby, she does not like Las Vegas very much. She does not have a lot of friends there, and with everything that happened with the bad cops last year, well, we are both ready to move. We will have brand new start and a brand new baby!"

I laughed. "Good. I was worried. Me and Mickey, we want you there. We wouldn't be good just the two of us. We need you as a partner."

"You and Mickey are very good, just the two of you."

"Yes! But not in the business. It'll be better with three."

Luis paused. "Ah. You think I will take your side when there is a disagreement?"

I frowned. "Well, not always, I guess, but sometimes, anyway."

"No comment, *amiga.*" Luis turned on the radio and The Shins came on, one of Portland's famous homespun bands.

I pulled up in front of the house and locked the car. We both walked up the steps. I had the house key ready, when Luis motioned with his hand for me to stop, and then held a finger to his lips.

The front door was ajar.

"They probably just left it open, Luis," I whispered, trying to convince myself as much as him.

He kept one hand up and with the other picked up a smooth stone that was sitting on the porch. Dad often kept rocks that he found while gardening. This one had a surprisingly regular oval shape and was smooth all around, but for one pointed end.

We tiptoed in, me behind Luis, and I heard whimpering. Dusty.

I made my way quietly to the coat closet and opened the door. She came out, wagging her tail and her butt like nobody's business and leaned against me, wanting pets.

"They would never put her in the closet," I whispered again, my voice considerably shakier this time.

Luis crept to the den, found his bag, and pulled out his gun and clip. He loaded it and indicated that I should take Dusty outside. I shook my head. He frowned and pointed at the door, but I insisted.

"Dusty could help. She helped out last time." Dusty had kept a firm hold on a very bad man's leg during the siege at my parents' house in California.

Luis turned away and started going through the house, room by room, with me and Dusty behind him. Upstairs, nothing. Backyard, nothing. My parents were nowhere to be found.

Luis laid his gun on the coffee table downstairs, sat on the couch, and let out a breath of relief. "Perhaps we are overreacting. Could they have simply gone for a walk?"

I slid onto the couch. "And leave Dusty in the closet? No. This is weird. They wouldn't do that." Dusty plopped her head on my lap and gazed at me with her adoring eyes.

Then I saw a business card on the coffee table. It wasn't there that morning. I picked it up by the edges and gasped.

"Amiga?"

I handed it to Luis.

It read, "Loren Scranton, CPA."

Chapter Thirteen

It's an odd situation, when you don't know if it's dire or innocent. I was trying not to be alarmed, but missing parents with a dog in the closet...that's just plain alarming. Still, I was hesitant to call the police. We'd been seeing too much of them lately, and I kept thinking about my parents' behavior the previous morning. Maybe they had some big secret. Maybe they left in a hurry and forgot to shut the door. Maybe Dusty liked being put in the closet.

I looked in there, to see if there were any doggie toys or treats or a doggie bed or food. I found a tennis ball, with remnants of doggie slime. Nothing else.

I picked up the stone that Luis had left on the futon when he traded it for his gun. It wasn't even pretty. An interesting shape, but rocks? My astrophysicist brilliant father?

Luis had gone outside to look around, saying he might approach some neighbors, see if they had seen Mom and Dad. I didn't know any of the neighbors. Did Mom and Dad know them?

I sat down on the floor with Dusty and studied Scranton's card, now in a ziplock bag. It was a little bit damaged, like it had been held too tightly in someone's hand. It told me nothing, except his address and phone number.

I jumped up and pulled out my phone. I would call this creepoid wine-spilling stalker and demand that he tell me what the hell was going on or it would be a long day in hell the next time he saw me, I tell you what. My hands were shaking as I started to hit the numbers.

Then I stopped, because I looked out the window and saw Mom and Dad, laughing, while they followed Luis up to the house from across the street.

I dropped the phone and flung the front door open. "What the hell! What happened?! Where were you? I thought you were kidnapped, or dead, or running for your lives, or…"

Mom pulled up short, but Dad sprinted up the stairs and took me in his arms. "Muffinhead, we're so sorry. We were gone just a few minutes. Stopped to see our neighbors. We must have left the door open by mistake."

"Dusty was in the CLOSET!"

Dad nodded. "Let me show you something." He led me to the closet and called Dusty over. "Open, girl. Open."

Dusty finagled her paw along the bottom of the door and it popped open. Then she waddled inside and did the same thing, shutting it behind her.

Dad beamed. "Good girl!" he praised her through the closed door. Then, to me, "I taught her that trick! The only problem is, she can't seem to open the door from the inside, for some reason. I've never known her to do this unless she's performing it as a trick. I'll have to put some sort of latch on here…." His voice faded out when he opened the door, and Dusty emerged, wiggling and wagging all around us.

Mom and Luis had come in, but Mom wasn't beaming. "Jeff." She got Dad's attention.

"What is it, Syl?"

She put her arm around me. "The business card? Luis told me."

I handed it over to Dad. "He was here. The dirtbag was here. Must have walked right in because you guys are too happy-go-lucky these days to close and lock your front door."

Dad took a look at it and gave it to Mom, who only glanced at it before she handed it to me. "Darling, we're sorry we scared you. But I don't understand this. We were gone maybe twenty minutes, tops. Why would he come here, come inside, drop off a card, and leave?" Mom turned to Luis.

"Folks, I see this as two possibilities. One is good. One is bad."

"How can this be good, Luis?" I asked. "I mean, how does he even know where Mom and Dad live? He saw us in the Pearl the other day, and now he's followed us to the house? It's way too creepy." I shuddered.

Mom suddenly looked ill, scrunching up her mouth and closing her eyes. "I told him."

"WHAT?"

"When he and I chatted at the airport, I told him where we lived."

"THE ADDRESS??"

Her eyes were still closed. "Well, not exactly, but the name of the street, and that we were behind the Sunshine Bakery, and, oh shit."

"WHAT?"

"Annabelle, please stop yelling at me." She took a breath. "I mentioned that Jeff had planted a beautiful garden in the front with a Japanese maple tree."

I sat down. "You told a complete stranger this in the baggage claim area of an airport? Did you hand over your social security number, too, along with your mother's maiden name?"

"*Amiga,* please, your mother did nothing wrong. She is friendly, that is all. People talk about their houses and their gardens."

Dad agreed. "Absolutely right, Syl, none of this is your fault."

I rubbed my face. "Luis, what is the good thing that this could mean? His being here?"

"He could be innocently looking for you both for reasons we do not know."

"Good thought," said Dad. "Entirely possible."

"Right," I said. "Or he's tracking us down about the gun and the backpack. Maybe he hurt Claudia. Maybe he killed Hank Howard or Howard Hanks or whatever his name is."

Luis sat down next to me. "If he meant great harm, Annabelle, would he have left a calling card?"

I leaned against him. "Probably not, unless he left it as a threat."

Luis hugged me and kissed the side of my head. "If that is what he is doing, he is a very foolish man. He has more to worry about than any of us."

"I was going to call him. Do you think I should?"

Luis shrugged. "I say we ignore him."

"I like you, Luis!" exclaimed my mother, who was heading toward the kitchen. "You are welcome here any time, any day, all the time!" I heard her open the refrigerator. "Jeff, dear, will you open this? We should celebrate!"

I turned around to see my mother holding out a bottle of champagne. Four flutes were already positioned on a tray on the counter.

Dad smiled and did a little dancey walk over to her. They kissed, and he started unwrapping the foil at the top of the bottle.

I stood up and threw my hands in the air. "What the fuck are we celebrating? You people are crazy! We have big problems here, and you want to drink champagne?" I envisioned spending the rest of my time in Portland talking to elder-care facilities.

Luis, frowning, stood up, too.

Dad popped open the bubbly and motioned us to come to the kitchen, while he poured. "We have big news, Bea. Just found out this afternoon that it's all set, so we can tell you about it now."

He handed each of us a glass, then took one for himself and raised it. We followed suit, though for me and Luis, the motion was halfhearted at best.

"Your mother and I, Bea, are about to embark on a great adventure. We've invested in a new business, with Sal and Drew, across the street." He paused to kiss Mom. "We are the proud owners of the Sunshine Bakery!"

I was too stunned to drink. My mouth was agape. Luis and my parents clinked glasses and sipped. I stayed frozen.

"Honey? Come on now, this is exciting news!" My mother was all aglow.

"Mom." I put my glass down. "You don't cook, let alone bake. You know nothing about business, and by the way, neither do you, Dad. And who are Sal and Drew? Tell me why this is good news! The world does not need dry muffins, bland cakes, rock-hard cookies, and banana bread that is more like banana gushy!"

Mom laughed like that was the funniest thing she ever heard. Dad gave me an oh-you-are such-a darling-daughter look. "You mother will not bake. Sal and Drew bake. We're simply investors. We like them. You will, too. In fact, they've invited us over for dinner tonight!"

"And, Miss Nervous Nellie, I have decided to walk away from the hospital for good—but I'll sue them to pay out my contract, those fucks—and take on more hours at the clinic. So I'll be plenty busy."

I picked up my champagne and chugged it. "I am happy for you, I think. I don't know. This has been a very strange afternoon." I put the empty glass down. "I'm going to take a nap. Then Luis and I have to go to the Uptown Billiards Club, to follow up on a lead. So I don't know if we can make dinner."

Luis coughed. "Annabelle, I think we can go to that club after dinner. It would not be a good thing to decline the invitation, do you think?"

I regarded the three of them, and just one thing rang through my head, loud and clear: *Mickey, please get your ass out here.*

Chapter Fourteen

I was totally out of sorts. I lay down on the bed upstairs and tried to breathe deeply while studying the ceiling, which had absolutely nothing to offer beyond white space. I pulled out my phone and dialed Mickey. No answer. I left him a message. "They're buying a bakery, Mickey. We're drinking champagne and they're buying a friggin' bakery while Loren Scranton was inside their house. Dusty can open closet doors. Where are you?" I hung up.

I rolled onto my side and eventually fell asleep. I dreamed about me and Dusty finding our way through a strange house, looking for I don't know what, while my mother followed us, covered in flour.

Dad woke me up, jostling me gently. "Bea, time to wake up. We're expected at Sal and Drew's."

I opened my eyes. Dusty was staring right into them, across the top of the bed. "Okay, Dad." I pushed myself up to sitting and patted Dusty on the head. "Dad, really, a bakery?"

"You'll see, muffin. You'll like our neighbors. Good people. And I promise, neither your mother nor I will do any of the actual baking. I am looking forward to sprucing the place up a bit."

I rubbed my eyes. "Maybe we should go there in the morning for pastries?"

He shook his head. "No, it's closed as of yesterday until we have a grand opening." His eyes sparkled.

"Dad, um, have you forgotten that you're an astrophysicist?"

He smiled. "Hell, darling, I'm just Jeff Starkey, when all is said and done." He winked at me. "Wash your face, put on some shoes, and let's go." He left.

I did what he told me to do. In fact, it's hard to recall any time in my life when I didn't do what my father asked. He and I have a strong unspoken bond. I never had the urge to rebel against him. He was always calm and reasonable, whereas my doctor mother was excitable and outspoken and, more times than I liked to remember, embarrassing. Dad, no, he was reliable. Dependable.

I changed my clothes to look a little nicer for the new business-partner neighbors. While I was dressing in black slacks and a silky bright blue top, Mom called up to me that they were heading over with Luis and I should just come as soon as I was ready. "It's the gray house with the green trim, right across the street."

I brushed on mascara, checked my phone for messages from Mickey, sent him a text (R U OK? I am a little worried) and headed downstairs and out the front door. I carefully locked it with the key Dad had given me.

I rang the doorbell and a handsome man—in his forties, I figured—answered. I held out my hand. "You must be Drew. Hi, I'm Annabelle, Sylvia and Jeff's daughter…"

"Annabelle!" He grabbed my hand, led me inside, and hugged me. "It is so good to meet you! But no, I'm Sal. Drew's inside with your folks and Luis. What a charmer he is, right? Can you both move out here so that we can have endless nights of wine, song, and games? I mean it, your parents are the greatest, and now I can tell already that you are, too, and when will we meet Mickey, who I understand is quite the macho man?"

I stared at him. Then I laughed. Then he laughed and let me go. "Right. We're gay. They didn't tell you."

"No! It's a pleasure, truly! I'm all yours!"

He led me by the hand into the living room, where Drew jumped up and gave me a similar greeting. "What's your poison, sweetheart?"

"Bourbon."

We all settled in around the coffee table, which presented an astonishing array of cheeses, nuts, fruit, crackers, olives, and sliced bell peppers. The conversation was lively, to say the least. We were talking over each other, finishing each other's sentences, and laughing luxuriously. Even Luis, who is usually so self-contained, seemed looser than I had ever seen him. Drew even talked him into a second beer—a rarity for Luis.

As for me, I was getting slightly bombed. Two bourbons, and I was loopy. By the time we sat down to dinner, I was guzzling Pellegrino, trying to regain my equilibrium. We all marveled at the perfectly cooked pasta with asparagus, in a light lemony cream sauce, and the warm, home-baked bread, and the crisp arugula salad. I found myself relaxing, really relaxing, for the first time since I arrived in Portland.

Sal and Drew, both great cooks, told me about the bakery, and how the previous owners simply were ready to retire, and they jumped at the chance to buy it. Drew was a high-school English teacher and didn't make a lot of money. Sal was an actor, who had made some bucks in voice-overs and advertising, but was mostly in love with indy films. They told me they were smart with their money (they sure knew how to find beautiful furniture and fixings in thrift stores), but needed other partners for the bakery business. Enter Sylvia and Jeff, as giddy with the new enterprise as Sal and Drew were for each other.

I liked them so much that I dropped my reservations about my parents becoming local merchants. But after they served their homemade éclairs for dessert (holy moly!), I begged their forgiveness for cutting out early. I was woozy with booze and sugar and I wanted to call Mickey.

They insisted that Mom and Dad and Luis stay for a while to play poker; apparently it had become a bit of a ritual of late (when did my parents ever play poker?). I had never imagined Luis as a poker player, but he did come from Las Vegas, so, whatever.

I kissed everyone good-bye, reminded Luis that we had to head over to the billiards club later, and closed the front door behind me. I gently descended their stairs to the street and looked over at my parents' house.

And froze.

Someone was sitting on the front porch.

A man, I could tell, by the overcoat and the fedora-style hat.

I ducked behind a tree and peered around it.

The man was fiddling with something, maybe his phone. I hadn't turned the porch lights on, so it was hard to see.

I adjusted my position. He pulled out a pack of cigarettes and was about to light one, when I darted out from the tree and ran across the street.

"You don't smoke!" I yelled.

Mickey stood up and caught me as I flew into his arms.

"Only when I fly three thousand miles, worried sick about you, and don't find you home."

We kissed and kissed again. "You used to smoke?" I murmured.

"Mmm hmm."

"You're not starting up again?" I kissed him.

"No. Just a moment of weakness. I'll throw them away."

"You found the boy?"

"Yes. Alive and well. I'll tell you all about it. You were across the street?"

"Mmm. Sal and Drew. Mom and Dad's new business partners. You'll love them. But you're not going to meet them right now."

He studied my face, a slight smile on his lips. "No? Why, do you have something else in mind?"

I brushed his black hair from his forehead and locked onto his dark brown eyes. "They're going to be playing poker over there for at least an hour, I figure."

He smiled, picked me up, took the front door key from my hand, and carried me over the threshold as effortlessly as Richard Gere spirited Debra Winger out of the factory in *An Officer and a Gentleman*, with all of her coworkers clapping and cheering. We didn't have an audience, but then, we didn't want one.

It was blissful to be lying naked in bed with Mickey, snuggled up against him, listening to him tell me about the missing kid. "It was my last lead. A duplex in Queens. I sat in the Mustang for three hours, waiting for someone to come in or out. Then, bingo, I see an older kid, tall and skinny, come up the sidewalk with a messenger bag over his shoulder."

"You knew who it was?"

"I wasn't sure, but he looked like the older brother. So I came up behind him as he was entering the building and grabbed him. I forced him inside, and there was Matthew, sitting on the floor in the living room watching a Transformers movie, eating tortilla chips."

"His brother took him?"

"Yeah. What a jerk. Roscoe. A twenty-year-old asshole. He told Matthew that their parents were going away for a while and that Matthew was to stay with him."

"Why?"

"Roscoe has daddy issues. Wanted to freak out his parents."

"Why didn't Matthew call his parents? He must have had access to a phone. Didn't he see his picture on the news?"

"He was having a pretty good time. No school, watching movies, hanging out with his cool older brother, who kept him away from any news. Matthew didn't know he was a missing person. Anyway, I cuffed Roscoe and called the parents and the police."

"What about the police? Why couldn't they find him?"

"I was lucky. Roscoe moved around a lot. He has money. He's good at hiding his trail."

I snuggled closer. "I don't think you were lucky. I think you were a brilliant Asta Investigations private eye."

"Hmm. As it turned out, I solved two cases at once. Roscoe was dealing drugs. He was shipping them in puppets."

I propped myself up on my arms and looked at him. "Puppets?"

Mickey laughed. "Stuffed animal puppets. I found a couple of them in his messenger bag."

I shrieked. "With cocaine hidden inside?"

He pulled me back down on the bed next to him. "Yes. I got a call tonight. Apparently Roscoe used all sorts of warm and fuzzy animals. Teddy bears, and polar bears, and lions and tigers and penguins and kitty cats and…"

"Bonkers! How's *my* kitty?"

Mickey kissed me. "Fine. Vicki in the downstairs flat is watching over him. They get along famously. He yowls out by the fire escape window and she calls up to him, "Bonks! I love you!"

I giggled. "He's such a flirt." I glanced at the clock. "We have to get up and go to the billiards club. Luis will probably be home any minute." I rolled away from Mickey and jumped out of bed. "Ready to rock and roll?"

"What, again?" he answered, with a smirk.

Chapter Fifteen

Tipsy Mom fell all over Mickey when he opened the door for her, Dad, and Luis. Dad gave him a man hug, and Luis held him like a long-lost brother. I was happier than the ending of an awful, sappy Hallmark movie. Name one, any one, if you can. It doesn't matter.

I had sobered up considerably, having, um, exercised with Mickey, followed by gulping down three espressos from my parents' machine. So I didn't allow for much greeting time. "Hey, boys, it's time to go play some pool. Let's *vamos*."

Luis laughed. "*Amiga*, you speak just like a native."

I knew he was kidding. "*Bueno*. Chop chop."

"Annabelle, darling, what is your hurry? That place will be open for at least another couple of hours, and, holy crap, Mickey just got here, and I think we should all chat for bit, don't you, Mickey?" Mom squeezed his hand.

"Sylvia, there's nothing I would rather do than sit and chat, but my partners here, it's their case, and they're in charge. We'll have lots of time tomorrow." He kissed her hand.

"He's a keeper, Bea." Mom beamed at me, and then back at Mickey. It was enough to make me hurl.

"Um, Mom, I know. I live with him, remember?" I traded glances with Dad, who smiled his usual calm, it's-all-okay smile. "Really, Mickey, Luis, let's get out of here." I picked up Dad's car keys from the counter and jingled them. "Okay with you, Dad?"

He nodded. "Be careful, have fun, maybe Mickey should drive? You've had a couple?"

I considered this, then tossed the keys to Mickey. "Sure. I'll navigate. *Hasta la vista!*"

Mickey disengaged from Mom, Luis shook Dad's hand, and I hustled out. I heard Luis say, "Thank you, Jeff. We will take good care of the car and of your daughter," and Mickey echo him with, "Yes, we will. No worries there."

I was ruffled. *Do I want my friends to take care of me?* I thought. *Sure, and I hope they think I take care of them, too. But if I'm a partner in this operation, then why is it that I am the one everyone assumes needs to be taken care of? I mean, I have acted swiftly in situations that have called for it. I'm nervy and strong and I can run fast, and I fired a gun once when I had to, and while I don't want to ever do that again, I would if I had to. So what is this taking care of the little missus thing because...?*

"Annabelle?"

"Huh?"

"You're mumbling to yourself." Mickey was waiting for me to get in the passenger side of the car.

I opened the door and got in. Then I turned to face him and Luis, who was in the backseat. "Look, I love you both, and you both love me, right?"

They nodded.

"And we're partners?"

They nodded again.

"And we take care of each other, right?"

More nodding.

"So you don't have to tell my father that you will take care of me."

"Babe, it's just a nice thing to say to your father. No big deal." Mickey stuck the key into the ignition.

Luis leaned forward. "Annabelle, we trust you and we depend on you."

"I'm not a little girl."

Mickey laughed. "I should hope not."

"You know what I mean, Mickey. I don't want to be condescended to."

He reached over and patted my knee. "Okay. I get it."

"I'm an equal partner."

"*Sí*," said Luis.

I looked at Mickey, expecting a response. He paused. "You will be an equal partner, once you have more experience and get a license. Come on, Annabelle, you haven't been trained as a police officer. You don't know very much about detective work. You have good instincts, and you're gutsy. That's more than half the battle, but you still need experience. And partners protect each other, and Luis and I will always protect you."

"Okay. I get that. And I'll prove my worth to both of you, you'll see."

Mickey put his hand behind my neck and pulled me toward him. "Hon, you already have. Really, this is not an issue." He kissed me. "Let's go find out if so-called Hank Howard was a regular at the Uptown Billiards Club. Do you have a picture of Claudia?"

"Yup." I patted my purse. "Let's *vamos*."

Luis chuckled.

The Uptown Billiards Club is located on the edge of the Pearl District. It's another Portland night spot with an old-fashioned feel that's authentic and cool. A small dining room offers seating for a couple dozen patrons, while a long bar lines a big room with several pool tables. The place was hopping when we got there.

We didn't start asking questions right away. Instead, because it was late, we saw a free table and I racked up the balls. Mickey and Luis were about to discover that I have a suppressed pool-shark alter ego. I like to call her "Ripley," after Sigourney Weaver's lead character in *Alien*. Ellen Ripley could kick anyone's ass, even disgusting out-of-space monsters that can hatch in humans' stomachs.

Come to think of it, maybe that movie had something to do with me not wanting babies.

Luis chalked his cue and broke, got one in and missed on his next shot. Then Mickey hit one in and missed on his second shot. And then, wow, it was one of the best moments of my life. I ran the table. I was on fire, so much so that other people took notice and watched. Mickey couldn't take his eyes off me. I figured he was about to get down on his knees and ask me to marry him, the way he was looking so in awe. Luis grinned and chatted with the bystanders.

After I gently nudged the eight ball into the far corner pocket, I threw my arms straight up in the air and laughed. A biker-type dude came up to me and asked me if I'd play him. He was a little drunk, and he got too close to me. I saw Mickey start toward me as I graciously declined. "No. Back off, now, or your nuts will find their way to your Adam's apple." Biker dude sneered at me and turned away, just as Mickey got to me.

I put my hands on my hips and smiled. "Coming to my rescue?"

"Yes, and not ashamed to say it. What did you say to him?"

"Not important. Want to play another game?" I put my arm around his waist and grinned.

"Several more games, all kinds of games, all the time. But let's have a drink now, see what we can learn, Minnesota Fats."

"Call me Ripley."

We made our way to the bar and ordered three beers. The bartender plopped the bottles down in front of us. "Nice shooting, sister," she said. She was small—petite, even—but wiry-strong and multi-tattooed with rose branches snaking up and down her arms.

"Thanks." I tipped my bottle toward her and took a swig. "Nice place here. We're from New York and Las Vegas."

"Come back anytime. It's fun to have good women players in here."

"What's your name?" asked Mickey.

"Greta."

We introduced ourselves, and then clinked glasses while Greta left to wait on other customers.

"Annabelle, you have many hidden talents, is what I think," said Luis.

"Well, I just exposed the best one."

"I'm not so sure about that." Mickey whispered in my ear, then kissed it with just a touch of tongue. I shivered down to my toes.

"Get a room," said a deep voice behind us.

We turned around to see Biker Dude, too close, again. Before either of us could respond, he grabbed the top of each of our shoulders and pushed us down on the bar. Greta got to us quickly, but Luis was even faster. In a second he was off his bar stool and on the gorilla's back, pulling him off of us. Like he was a bouncer for the place, Luis shoved Biker Dude's right arm in a hammerlock and ushered him toward the door. People made a path for him, and I could hear him say, "Do you understand what I am saying to you? You should not come back tonight, because if you do, you will have many damaging things done to you, things I do not even want to talk about, they scare me too much." Someone opened the door, and Luis shoved the guy outside.

Luis sat back down after shaking a few hands, and swallowed some beer while Mickey and I smiled broadly.

Greta brought us all another round. "I owe you, mister. Julius there, he's a little, uh…overwrought. Thanks."

After a while the bar thinned out and Greta came to our end to chat a bit. This was the opportunity to find out what we had come there for in the first place. I pulled out the picture of Claudia. "Greta, do you know this girl? She's mixed up in something, and we're trying to help her."

"Cops? Really?"

Mickey shrugged. "Yes and no. Used to be cops. Now we're PIs."

She raised her eyebrows in a way that showed she was impressed. "No kidding? Never met a PI before." She studied the picture, then flicked her finger against it. "Nope, sorry. I don't recognize her."

"What about Howard Hanks?" I asked.

"You mean Hank Howard," Mickey corrected me.

Greta froze. "You know about Hank?"

"It looks like you do, too," said Mickey.

"He was murdered."

"Yes."

"Do you know who did it?" Greta's voice wavered.

"No."

"Were you friends?" I asked.

Greta smoothed her short blond hair and grabbed a rag to start wiping the bar. "He was my ex-boyfriend. I told the police all about him."

Luis rested his hand on Greta's, which was furiously rubbing at a spot. "We are very sorry about your loss. We do not mean to distress you in any way. Can you tell us, though, if Hank ever talked about someone named Claudia?"

She stared at him. "Huh? No." She backed up, away from the bar. "Hank wasn't all bad. He had drug problems back East. He was trying to go straight. We were talking about getting back together…What's this all about, with this Claudia chick?"

"She was mugged. There was a mix-up with a gun, it ended up with me by mistake…"

Mickey interrupted me. "Just one more question. Do you know a Wesley Young or Loren Scranton?"

Greta shook her head. "No. Look, I have to clean up here. You guys want anything else?"

"No. Thanks, Greta. We're sorry, really." I pulled out one of my business cards and tossed it on the bar. "We'll be in town for a few more days, in case you think of anything that might help us."

"Sure thing. " She didn't look at us.

Mickey dropped some cash for Greta, and we stood to go. I glanced over my shoulder as we were leaving to see her talking on her cell phone. It looked like she was reading my card to someone on the other end.

Chapter Sixteen

Mickey drove us home, with the help of my phone's GPS. There are about a half dozen bridges in Portland, linking the east and west sides of the Willamette River, and out-of-towners like us needed directions.

"Remember when we used fold-up maps?" I was watching us, the blue dot on my screen, move across the Burnside Bridge. "I could never refold them right."

"Damn it." Mickey got to the other side of the bridge and slowed down.

"What?"

"Police. Behind us. Pulling me over."

Luis and I turned around to see the blinking lights of a police car. "AGAIN? What the...?"

"Ssshh, *amiga*. Stay cool."

"How many beers did you have, Mickey?"

"Two. I'm fine." He got us across the bridge, pulled over, and put the car in park. We waited for the cop to approach, and Mickey rolled down his window. "What's the problem, Officer?"

"License and registration, please."

I dug the registration out of the glove compartment while Mickey dug in his wallet for his license. The policeman shined his flashlight in the car at all of us. I handed the registration to Mickey, and he passed it along to the cop with his license.

"Mr. Paxton?"

"Yes."

"Are you aware that you were driving erratically back there?"

"No, I wasn't aware of that."

"Have you been drinking?"

"Two beers in two hours."

"Would you get out of the car, please?"

Mickey paused, patted my knee, and got out. I turned to Luis. "What the fuck, Luis?"

He held his finger to his lips to shush me again, then rolled down his window so that we could hear better what was going on.

The policeman asked why Mickey was driving a car registered to Jeffrey Starkey, and then put him through the drunk driving test moves: following the officer's pen with his eyes, standing on one leg, walking in a straight line heel to toe. Mickey did just fine. The cop handed the documents back to him and said, "Drive carefully."

"Can you tell me what I did wrong?"

"Started to make a turn a couple of times, and then didn't."

"I'm visiting Portland. I wasn't sure which way to go."

"Sorry for the bother, Mr. Paxton. You and Beatrice have a good night."

Mickey froze. I knew because he had started to get into the car, but his hand stopped on the door handle. He let go and turned to face the policeman. "Beatrice? You know that's her name because...?"

The cop took a moment before answering. "The registration is listed under Starkey."

"And?"

"Listen, Mr. Paxton, I think it's best if you move along now. If you have any questions about this traffic stop, don't hesitate to contact my superiors." And with that, he turned and walked back to his squad car.

Mickey got in and pulled the door shut. "They're watching you."

"They think I'm involved."

"Or they think someone else is watching you, and they're protecting you."

"Which do you think?"

He turned the key in the ignition. "We'll meet with Dawson and Monroe tomorrow and find out."

Luis leaned forward between our front seats. "We do not want the police to be against us. We are police, we understand police. We knew two disreputable police in San Francisco and Las Vegas. But we cannot make assumptions that the new ones we meet, here or anywhere, are crooked."

I shrugged. "Either way, I don't like being followed."

Mickey pulled out onto the street to head home. I twisted around and watched the lights of the police car follow us for a block and then turn off.

"Babe, back there at the bar?"

"What?"

"Too much information, what you were telling Greta."

I took a breath and told myself that I had to learn to take criticism. "What, exactly?"

"I cut you off before you said any more about the gun. All she knows now is that you were in a mix-up with it. That alone might be too much. We know she was in a relationship with Hanks. We need to be careful about sharing information."

"So you want me to hold things closer to my chest."

Mickey smiled. "Sometimes, yes. Me included."

"Like *Señor* Julius said, get a room, you two," piped up Luis from the backseat.

Mickey and I were sitting up in bed together, rehashing the week's events. This much we knew: Claudia was supposed to be the recipient of the backpack with the gun in it. The gun was used to murder Hank Howard. I mean Howard Hanks. Whatever. Greta used to be his girlfriend. Claudia had a boyfriend named Wesley Young. Claudia's father is a jerk. Loren Scranton may or may not be involved. Police have put some sort of APB out to keep track of me.

"We really need to talk to Claudia. I wish she would wake up."

Mickey yawned. "That would be good. In the meantime, like I said, let's meet with the police, see where things stand with you, and then try to find this Wesley Young kid."

I leaned over and kissed him. "Go to sleep. I'm going downstairs to have some herbal tea. I'm all wound up like a pitcher in a batting cage."

Mickey snorted. "You and your convoluted sports metaphors."

I got out of bed. "Just throwing some curve balls to see if you can catch them."

"Stop it, please."

I slipped into my sweats. "Well, all right, but don't blame me if I make it around second while you're covering first."

Mickey hurled a pillow at me as I hustled out of the room.

I was sitting at the dining room table, leafing through a restaurant supply catalog and noting which pages had their corners turned down. Mom and Dad must have been shopping for stuff for the bakery. I saw cute little bistro tables and chairs circled with red ink. There was another page with flatware and one with dishes. This bakery thing was real. It still felt surreal to me.

The house was so quiet. I felt comfortable and at ease, now that both Mickey and Luis were with me. I was confident that together we'd find our way out of this quagmire. I washed my mug in the sink and cleaned Dusty's dish. Dusty. She was a good protector, too, sound asleep in my parents' bedroom.

I stretched and turned to head upstairs, when I stopped short.

I heard the back door open quietly behind me.

In the split second it took me to formulate the thought that the door wasn't locked, someone clapped a hand over my mouth and wrapped an arm around my chest and started dragging me to the door.

I struggled, but I couldn't release the grip.

Whoever it was held me so tightly I couldn't make enough noise to wake even Luis in the den.

In the backyard, another pair of hands grabbed my feet from behind and I was carried to the street and into the back of a van. They tossed me stomach-first onto a smelly mattress. One abductor positioned a blindfold over my eyes and duct-taped my hands behind my back.

I remembered to cross my wrists.

Then he rolled me over and held me while his partner slapped a strip of tape over my mouth, and bound my ankles together.

I saw no faces.

My kidnappers spoke not a word.

They drove the van east, while I tried to control my breathing.

I concentrated on Mickey, bringing his face clearly to my mind. *He would find me,* I thought. *Mickey and Luis. Liam Neeson has nothing on them in those* Taken *movies. Except a Roman nose.*

I was trying to fake myself out with false bravery. In reality, I was more frightened than a shortstop without a helmet.

Chapter Seventeen

The mattress kept me from rolling too far from side to side when the van turned corners, or from sliding toward the front when it came to a stop. I tried to concentrate on the direction of the turns and the number of stops. I started counting off seconds in my head, too, so that when we got to wherever we got, I could estimate how long it took to get there. Plus I was trying to worm my way out of the blindfold and the tape.

The blindfold was easier. I was able to roll onto my side and rub my face against the mattress, easing the cloth down my nose enough to see.

Pitch black. No windows. That had to mean the back of the van was a separate compartment from the front.

I couldn't see the kidnappers, but they couldn't see me either.

I gave up on the directions, but kept counting, probably too fast. I started working on freeing my hands. Because I had crossed my wrists, I could maneuver them into a looser position. I twisted and turned them back and forth, trying to wrench one hand free, all the while counting. *Seven hundred twenty-two. Seven hundred twenty-three. Seven hundred twenty...*

I yanked my right hand out from behind me. "Take that, Houdini," I muttered, grateful for the self-defense class I took in New York where I learned that tip. I pulled the blindfold off and freed my left hand, ripped the tape off my mouth in one quick move without screaming, and unwrapped my ankles. I rubbed my wrists, red and scraped from the tape, and huddled on the floor.

Now what?

Seven hundred forty-seven. Seven hundred forty-eight.

The van exited the freeway. I had no idea of the direction it was heading anymore. Several turns later, it slowed down considerably and made a hard left. I figured we had reached our destination.

I crouched by the side of the two back doors, feeling for the hinges on each. They opened outward. I had two things in my favor. One was the element of surprise. All I could hope to do was to bust out of there as soon as a door opened.

Running fast was the other thing.

Except that I was wearing heavy socks. No running shoes.

And flannel pajamas.

I changed my position so that I was balanced on my butt, with my legs bent and in the air, my feet close to the doors, and my arms supporting me behind my back.

I heard footsteps, and took a deep breath.

When the door opened I jabbed my legs straight out with as much force as I could muster and was lucky to connect with the face of one of the kidnappers.

"Fuck!" he yelled as he fell to the ground.

The other guy wasn't there.

I jumped out and fled down the driveway of what looked like an industrial warehouse. I heard the guy on the ground shout, "Jules! She's getting away!" I turned slightly to see the other coming from the building, where I guess he had gone to unlock the door while his partner was getting his kisser kicked.

I rallied all the speed I could, racing like Francois Cluzet, the lead character in the French film based on the Harlan Coben novel *Tell No One,* when the police are chasing him because they suspect him of murder.

Favorite movie scenes can be truly inspiring for saving one's ass. Trust me.

I cut through parking lots, crossed streets, and found myself in a wooded area, where I stopped to catch my breath and pull off some pebbles stuck to my socks, which were soaked from the damp ground. My feet were killing me, but I sprinted off again.

I ran and ran until I eventually reached what seemed to be a major road. It was so late, there was no traffic, but this would be my best bet. I crossed it to see what was over its far ledge.

I leaned over, resting my hands on my legs while I panted and gazed at the mighty Columbia River.

I was somewhere in north Portland, and if I remembered correctly, not all that far from the airport.

A car had to come by soon.

I wrapped my arms around myself, shivering.

Jules. Julius. Biker Dude.

"Fuck you, Greta!" I screamed it over and over, louder and louder, until I was exhausted.

That's when a truck saw me and pulled over. It was a semi. The driver rolled down the passenger window and yelled out to me. "Hey, you all right? You need a ride?"

I wasn't climbing into any more vehicles with strangers that night. "Would you make a phone call for me? Then my friend can come and pick me up?"

"Sure, but you're going to freeze out there in the meantime. Don't you want to get in…?"

"Please? Just the phone call." I gave him Mickey's cell number. He called and then hung up. He reached behind him, grabbed a blanket, and tossed it out the window to me. "I'll sit right here in the truck until he gets here. Okay with you?"

I nodded. "Thank you." Most of me wanted to climb inside to get warm, but an insistent nagging bit of me was not going to risk in any measure ending up like William Macy's wife in *Fargo*—kidnapped and dead.

Mickey sat in the backseat with me. Dad was driving, Luis was in the passenger seat. Mickey held me close while I tried to direct Dad to where I thought the warehouse was. But a lot of the buildings in the industrial park looked the same, and there was no sign of the van. We pulled into a parking lot.

"Sorry," I said. "I'm not sure anymore. It was dark, and I was running."

"Shall we wait here, call the police, tell them to meet us out here?" Dad asked, looking at Mickey in the rearview mirror.

Mickey rubbed my arm. "Annabelle's so cold."

"I'm warming up. The trucker's blanket was a big help. What a nice guy, huh? Thanks for thinking to bring my jacket and my sock-monkey hat, Dad."

He twisted the mirror so that he could see me, and smiled weakly. "Nothing to thank me for, Bea. That back door was unlocked. I can't believe I didn't check it."

"Any of us could have checked it, Jeff," said Luis. "It is not your fault."

Dad didn't respond.

"Call the police, Mickey. Are they looking for me already, or are they with Mom, or...?"

"I'll call." Mickey got out of the car, and I saw him pull a cigarette out of his pocket and light it.

Dad saw it, too. "Mickey smokes?"

"News to me, too. Apparently he used to, and now he does under stressful situations, although I never saw him smoke in Las Vegas. Did you, Luis?"

Luis shook his head. *"Nunca."*

Now, I'm not a no-smoking Nazi. I like it that restaurants and airplanes and nail salons aren't filled with tobacco smoke these days, but if someone wants to smoke without blowing the fumes all over me, who am I to judge them? I mean, we all have our addictions.

I tugged my sock-monkey hat tightly over my ears. "Greta's involved, Luis. I'm pretty sure that one of the kidnappers was Julius. She must have had him follow us home."

Luis shifted around in his seat. *"Amiga,* she seemed glad that I threw him out."

"She lied about everything, I'm sure of it. I told you, she made a phone call while we were leaving. Probably told him to follow us."

"Makes sense, but why kidnap you?"

We were all quiet for a while, waiting for Mickey to hang up. He did, then stubbed out his smoke on the pavement, and pocketed the butt before getting back in the car.

"Cool."

He frowned. "Smoking? It's so not cool."

I slipped my arm into the crook of his elbow. "No, that you picked up the butt. I hate litterbugs."

Luis suddenly sat up straight. "Greta. You said she lied about everything."

"No reason to trust her at this point."

"You remember, she said that she spoke to the police?"

"Yes."

"But remember, *amiga*, Perry at The Rowdy Yeats? He said that he had only just remembered that Hank Howard told him that he liked a girl at the Uptown Billiards Club."

"Uh huh. He did."

"So, he didn't tell the police that. The police wouldn't have even talked to Greta." Luis looked from me to Mickey and to Dad, and then back at me.

Mickey snapped his fingers. "Excellent, Luis. Greta learned about the gun from us. She was clueless otherwise." He paused. "Maybe she sent Julius after you to get the gun. Figured you still have it."

Dad was silent through all of this, his head leaning against the headrest. I saw him adjust his glasses, and noticed his hand was unsteady.

"Dad. It's okay. We're making progress. I'm fine. We're all fine."

He held that hand in the air, signaling that he heard me. But it was still shaking.

Soon a police car rolled into the parking lot, and we all got out, me a little weak-kneed, Mickey and Luis tough and ready, and Dad looking like he had been hit by an age-inducing virus that infected him faster than you could say rheumatoid arthritis.

"Dad." I put my arm around his waist. "It's not your fault. I'm fine."

"It *is* my fault, but that's not the problem." He stopped and turned to me. "I just got a text from your mother. Loren Scranton called her on our home phone."

"What did he say?!"

"I'm not sure. But her text said she let him have it and hung up."

"Go, Mom."

"Right. But…"

"Are you worried that he's coming back to the house and we're not there?"

"No. She's gone over to Sal and Drew's."

"Good. So why do you look like you're about to pass out?"

Dad held his hand to his forehead. "Darling, do I really need to explain that to you? My daughter was kidnapped tonight, and my wife is being stalked. How are you so calm?"

I didn't know how to answer that. I just shook my head.

He took my hand. "Let's join the conversation with the police and Mickey and Luis, and then let's get the hell home."

We walked hand in hand the few steps to the others. When Mickey met my eyes, I thought I might lose it. But maybe for the first time in my life, my father seemed to be relying on *my* strength, and no way was I going to let him down.

Chapter Eighteen

Dawson and Monroe weren't on the case this evening. The officers who arrived were very accommodating and professional. I gave them a full statement with as many details as possible. I knew the van was dark green, but I hadn't been able to determine the make. Mickey and Luis told them all about Greta and Julius and suggested that they get in touch with Dawson and Monroe to fill them in on the case. They nodded, wrote everything down, and said they'd take a few turns around the area to see if they could spot the van.

I filled Mickey and Luis in on the way home about Loren Scranton. Dad drove a little too fast, but we didn't get pulled over.

When he parked in front of the house, we all jumped out and sprinted up the steps of Sal and Drew's, whose front windows were blazing with light. Before Dad could knock, the door flew open.

"Friends! Come in, come in. All is well. Sylvia is having some calming tea while Drew, I'm afraid, is wearing a path in our living room carpet, pacing like a caged tiger. He's quite upset, as we both are, you all getting such a scare."

We walked into the living room. As soon as Mom saw me she rushed to give me a hug. "My brave, brave daughter. Let me look at you. Are you hurt at all?"

I kept my arms wrapped tightly around her. "No, a few bruises, and I'm chafed from the duct tape, but I'm fine."

That's when I finally lost it. I started sobbing. "Are you okay?"

"I'm fit as a fucking fiddle and mad as a hatter. Don't you worry about me."

I wiped my eyes when I disengaged and looked around for Mickey. He was leaning against the doorway, watching me with the most mournful eyes I had ever seen.

"Sal, if you don't mind, do you have any more bourbon?" I asked.

"Bea, it's three o'clock in the morning. Are you sure you want a drink?" Dad sounded so tired.

"Very sure."

"Me, too." He smiled, and everyone managed a little laugh.

"Drinks all around. However, at this hour, I insist on brandy. Sit down everyone, and let's hash out this awful business." Sal was off to the kitchen.

Mickey stayed standing, easing his way around the room, following the conversation by squinting at whoever was talking. His cop demeanor was raging. I had seen it before.

"Drew has been telling me about a stalker he dealt with once," Mom said. "Terrible business."

"It was a long time ago. He was convinced I was corrupting his son." Drew fidgeted with the tie on his bathrobe. That's when I realized that of the seven of us, four were in sleepwear. Dad, Mickey, and Luis looked like slumber-party crashers.

"Like, you were a perv or something?" I asked.

"Sort of. It was because we had a discussion in class one day about pornography, how standards have changed, and while one might think a book is pornographic, another might deem it literature."

"Sounds like a class I would have liked to have taken in high school," Sal said, entering the room carrying a tray of brandy snifters. We each took one and sipped.

Drew continued. "This kid went home and told his father that he should let him read all of Henry Miller's books, because they were literature."

"Well, they are, right?" Mom asked.

"Today, yes, that's how they are considered. Originally, complete porno. Anyhoo, I told the father that it was a complicated issue but that I would be happy to meet with him."

Sal perched on the arm of the wingback chair where Drew was sitting. "He refused, thank goodness."

"Yes. Turned out he preferred to send threatening letters to me and try to get me fired."

"I don't think he has much in common with Scranton," muttered Mickey.

I flashed him a look that I hoped told him to cool it.

Drew took a large swallow of brandy and stood up. "Then he tried to assault Sal."

"Holy fuck!" exclaimed Mom.

Mickey's squinting was even more pronounced than before. I wondered if he could even see.

Sal waved his hand in front of his face. "Oh, Drew, really. You can be so dramatic. That bivalve did not mean to assault me." Drew plopped back down in the chair while Sal took over. "We were cooking together. I went outside to snip some basil leaves from our herb garden right when the jerk hurled a copy of Miller's *The Tropic of Cancer* at our door, and it hit me in the head."

I smiled. "Death by porno. Or literature."

"Yes, sugar. We got a restraining order, and he left us alone."

"What happened to the son?" Luis asked.

Drew grinned. "Got his MFA in creative writing. Served daddy-dear right." With that, he got up and poured himself some more brandy from the decanter on the tray. "Perhaps your stalker is only armed with weapons similar to books, Sylvia. We can hope so, anyway."

"Sylvia, what did Scranton say to you on the phone?" Dad asked.

"He said 'Hello, this is Loren Scranton,' and I said, 'You have a lot of nerve, you sick prick, calling at this hour, and I don't know why you're stalking me and my daughter, but don't you ever come in my house again or I'll drop you quicker than a fucking hot potato.' He didn't respond, so I hung up."

Drew clapped his hands. "That's our Sylvia! Well done, honey!"

I was watching Mickey, whose expression had not changed. He clearly found none of this amusing. He also looked exhausted. It dawned on me that he must have been awake for well over twenty-four hours by now.

I stood up. "I need to go to bed."

Dad joined me. "I think we all do. Sal, Drew, thank you for opening your home to Sylvia, and to us." He held up his brandy snifter as a toast and then downed its contents.

Sal and Drew hugged all of us, even Mickey, though his response was perfunctory. Then we all crossed the street and went home.

◇◇◇

Mickey and I were in bed. I was on my side, my head propped up on a couple of pillows, contemplating him. "You okay? You've been very quiet."

He was lying on his back with his arm folded over his eyes. "I'm okay. I need to sleep."

"You're going to quit smoking, right?"

"Never really started. I threw the rest of them in the garbage."

"Mick…"

"Not now, Annabelle. Let's talk in the morning."

I rubbed his chest. "Fine, but…"

He rolled over and turned me onto my back. He brushed my hair out of my face. "I thought you were dead."

I nodded. "I know."

"And now people are making jokes and telling silly stories."

"People handle things differently."

"Do you trust Sal and Drew?"

I nodded again. "I absolutely do. You will, too. I promise."

He kissed me, and then rolled onto his back, arm over his eyes again.

"What do you want to do tomorrow?" I asked.

"Fly to New York. With you."

"Can't do that, *compadre*. I'm wanted in these here parts. Others might say that I've got parts that are wanted."

"Don't try to cheer me up."

"*Bueno, hombre*, as long you understand that I'm not going to stop talking until you tell me one thing."

"What."

"That I did real good getting away from them outlaws." My voice choked on the last word.

Mickey quickly took me in his arms and held me. "Oh, God, I'm so sorry. Yes, of course, I'm so proud of you. You did everything right. You are brave and strong and quick thinking and quick running."

I nestled close to him. "Is it okay if you hold me for a while?"

"As long as you want, babe, as long as you want."

So I lay there awake, listening to Mickey's even breaths of deep sleep, staring at the white ceiling, afraid to close my eyes.

Chapter Nineteen

I did fall asleep and didn't wake up until noon the next day. It was raining, and I was enjoying the sound of the drops hitting the roof. I curled up tight under the duvet and watched the giant sequoia branches swaying in the wind outside the window.

Eventually I rolled out of bed, took a shower, combed my hair, brushed my teeth, and pulled on my sweats. I was achy and stiff and my feet were tender. I sauntered downstairs to find the house empty, except for Dusty, who was wagging her tail ferociously at the bottom of the stairs.

"Hey, you." I rubbed her ears and hugged her. "Where is everybody?"

In the kitchen I found a note. Mickey and Luis had gone to the police station. Mom and Dad were grocery shopping.

I made myself a triple espresso and sat down in the living room, my feet up on the coffee table. The rain was falling harder, but it still sounded comforting to me. I didn't feel like talking to anyone, or going anywhere. I felt like watching a movie.

I moved into the den and started sorting through my parents' DVD collection. I was happy to locate *Persuasion,* the Jane Austen story starring Ciaran Hinds and Amanda Root. It might be my favorite romance film of all time, and I have a huge crush on Ciaran Hinds, even though I can never remember how to pronounce his name. It's like that girl's name, Siobhan, which you would think would sound like "see-OB-han" but it's really "shiVAWN." Makes no sense.

I popped in the movie and lounged on the futon, which Luis had made up neatly, settling in for some good old-fashioned comfort.

Until the doorbell rang.

It then occurred to me that it was odd my family had left me alone.

Dusty barked and waggled up to the front door. I followed cautiously behind. "Who is it?"

"Sugar, it's me. Sal."

I opened the door. "Hi."

"What are you up to?"

"Watching *Persuasion*."

"Aaah, with that dreamboat Ciaran" (he pronounced it "Keeran") "Hinds as Captain Wentworth and that mousy but irresistible whatshername Root as Anne Elliot?"

I grinned. "Amanda. And, my feelings exactly."

"Want some company?"

I hesitated. "As long as…"

"You don't have to talk."

"Perfect. Come in."

Sal entered and I shut the door behind him, but not without first noticing a mug on the table by the porch chair, which held a blanket. "You've been on guard?"

"At your service, milady." He bowed. "The others are out doing things that need to be done. I heard the TV come on, knew you were up." He held out a bag. "Cookies. My special recipe."

I peeked inside. "Snickerdoodles?"

"The best." I took one and we retired to the den, where I reached for the remote to restart the movie, but paused. "I keep thinking about last night."

"That's to be expected, for heaven's sakes."

"Not just what happened to me, but this stalker dude. I don't know what we should do if he calls again."

"I doubt he will, since Sylvia cut him down to size on the phone last night."

"I don't understand why he was calling here so late."

Sal considered that for a moment. "I don't either. Maybe he was drunk and feeling desperate." He held out the bag of cookies to me. "Have another."

I took three.

Near the end of the movie, when Anne discovers Captain Wentworth's letter and runs after him in the street, Sal grabbed my hand. "This is it, kid. The moment we've been waiting for." Then they kissed, we both got weepy, and I ate another cookie.

That's when Mom and Dad walked in, laden with packages. "We're home, darlings!" Mom called.

She found us in the den, holding our breaths as Captain Wentworth makes the announcement at a party that he and Anne will be married. In unison, we spoke the heartless father's lines, "Anne? You want to marry Anne? Whatever for?" And then Sal yelled at the screen, "You bastard daddy!"

I had a new soul mate.

Mom set two bags on the floor by the futon. "For you, dear." She patted the top of my head. "We did more than grocery shop."

I opened the first one to reveal new flannel pajamas, a bathrobe, and slippers. "Oh, Mom, this is so nice."

"I knew you wouldn't want to put those others on again. I threw them out this morning. Open the other one."

I looked inside to find a big shoebox. "You didn't!"

"Mmmm. I did."

I pulled out the gray suede boots with the blue toes and heels. "Holy shit, Mother, to use your words, these are crazy beautiful!" I jumped up, forgetting how much the bottoms of my feet hurt, winced, and gave her a big hug. "I can't wait to wear them."

Sal picked up a boot. "*Trés élégant*, Syl. Perhaps we should decorate the bakery in some cowboy theme and all wear beautiful boots."

"That's a fucking terrible idea, Sal dear. Now, I'm going to help Jeff put the groceries away. Thanks for looking after Annabelle."

"Oh, honey. She looked after me, too." Sal gave me a kiss on the cheek. "I'm off. I'll watch movies with you any time. Just ring. And don't worry about Stalker Creep. He's as effective as Mr. Elliot. Weak, in the end. In the front, too, I imagine." I laughed and walked him to the door. "Anyway, he's no match for the Starkeys or those two gorgeous young men you have in your life."

When Sal was gone I found Dad in the kitchen, folding up the reusable grocery bags. "Muffinhead, how are you feeling?"

"I'm fine, Dad. Just a little sore. When did Mickey and Luis leave?"

"Same time as us, so it has been about three hours, I guess. No news?"

I shook my head. "They went to see Dawson and Monroe?"

"Yes, to make sure they knew about Greta and the kidnapping. They also were talking about tracking down that boyfriend of Claudia's, Wesley Young."

"Good. I'm going to get dressed and get busy myself."

Mom stopped trimming the flowers she bought. "And do what?"

"See Claudia. Will you come with me, Mom? Maybe you can take a look at her chart, just in case…"

"Darling, you should rest today. Watch another movie. What have you eaten besides Snickerdoodles? Let me heat up some soup."

"How about a sandwich? Then I can take it with me, if you drive."

Dad resumed folding the bags. "She's not going to change her mind, Syl. Might as well make that sandwich."

"Well, shit. All right. Go get dressed. I'll be ready to go when you come back."

We made it to the hospital without incident. Claudia looked the same, though I thought she had a little bit more color in her cheeks. That might have been wishful thinking.

Mom found a nurse and asked if she could see Claudia's chart. She said she was a doctor friend of Nancy and Phillip and was trying to reassure them that everything was being done for their daughter. The nurse listened to all of this patiently and replied, "You can't see the chart if you're not her guardian." Then she walked away.

Back in Claudia's room, Mom pouted. "I'd never make a detective. I don't know how to lie to get people to tell me things."

"What are you talking about? You got patients in the ER to reveal their innermost darkest secrets and promise you their firstborns!"

She laughed. "It's easier when you're saving someone's life."

I opened the drawer in the bedside table. "I want you to look at this note, Mom. I know we showed you a picture of it, but I want your opinion on the handwriting."

"Crap, honey, I'm not a handwriting expert."

"I know, but I have a funny feeling about it, that it's too neat. Tell me what you think." I reached inside the drawer. "That's weird."

"What."

"It's gone." I searched again to make sure and closed the drawer.

"Would the police have taken it?"

I shrugged. "Don't know. I wonder who has visited her. Like maybe…"

"That bad boyfriend?"

I nodded. "Let's talk to another nurse this time."

We approached the nurses' station in the hall and I stopped a uniformed young woman, who was grabbing her purse. "Excuse me, could we talk to you about Claudia Bigelow? Nothing confidential. We're friends, and…"

"Sure, I guess so. I'm heading to the cafeteria, if you want to join me."

"That sounds great!" Mom was way too peppy.

The three of us aimed for the elevator. "I sure hope Claudia wakes up. She has a lot to live for."

"I'm sure she does," I said, "but what do you mean, exactly?"

"That boyfriend of hers? He's been here after visiting hours a few nights. He holds her hand and cries. He loves her SO much."

The elevator doors opened and we stepped inside. "Wesley, you mean?"

She nodded. "Yes. He's a hunkadoris."

"Holy shit," said Mom.

◇◇◇

We had coffee with Tiffany the nurse, who told us that even though the police had instructed the staff to keep an eye on Claudia's visitors, she didn't think it was anyone's business who Claudia was in love with and besides, it was clear that Wesley really, really loved her because she saw him crying once.

I tried to explain to her that there were lots of reasons for crying, like feeling bad that you hit your girlfriend so hard that she was lying in a coma.

"Not Wesley. Uh uh. I have a seventh sense about this stuff." Tiffany focused on a text that just announced itself with a bell on her phone.

"What's your sixth sense?" I placed the palm of my hand over her phone's screen.

"Huh?" She yanked her phone away.

"How old are you, dear?" Mom asked.

"Twenty-seven."

"And you're a nurse? Really?" I was amazed, not because of her age, but because she was so dumb.

She stared at me, all offended.

Mom took over. "Tiffany, when does Wesley usually show up?"

"I don't know. I've seen him only late at night, when I'm on that shift." She checked her screen again. "Anyway, I have to go now. Bye." She was dialing someone as she left us.

"Annabelle, why don't the police have someone stationed outside of Claudia's door, for chrissakes?"

"They can't provide protection for everyone who gets mugged. It's not like Claudia is a foreign dignitary or a mob boss or a movie star."

We finished our coffees and took the elevator to the parking garage. "I suppose we'll have to do our own stakeout for Wesley Young."

Mom was about to open the car door. "Not tell the police? We should tell the police that he has been coming here."

I shook my head. "We'll tell Mickey and Luis. I bet you the police will be happy to have two out-of-town policemen/PIs sit in the hospital hall for a couple of nights.

"And you?"

"I just might join them. I'd like to check in with Nancy and Phillip, though. See what they may have heard or seen."

We got in Mom's car, a new light blue Smart car. "This is the doggone cutest little car I've ever seen," I said.

"Why are you talking like John Wayne?"

"I guess these boots are made for talkin'." I brought an ankle up to rest on my knee, which wasn't easy in that car, and stroked my new gray boot.

"Big mistake, that. Buying those for you."

We pulled out of the parking place and drove down the hill while I called Mickey.

◇◇◇

We met Mickey and Luis downtown at the bar at Jake's Grill and ordered beers. They filled us in on their meeting with Monroe and Dawson about the previous night. The detectives were going to pay Greta a visit and find out more about Julius or Jules. The van hadn't been located, though I hadn't given them much to go on there.

"Let's say Greta killed Hank or got Julius to do it. Somehow she hears that Claudia needs a gun, so she arranges for the drop. Then we show up and she learns that the gun ended up with Annabelle. So Annabelle is kidnapped in order to get the gun back." Mickey took a swig of beer.

"Is this another way of telling me I should have kept my mouth shut around Greta?" I took two swigs of beer.

"No. Well, I wish you had, and then hadn't been kidnapped, but that's not why I brought all of this up. It seems that things are falling into place. If the police find Greta and Julius, that part of the puzzle will be solved. I doubt that Loren Scranton is involved. Maybe he's somehow obsessed with Sylvia, but we'll put that to rest eventually…"

"That weasly dickbrain," Mom interjected.

"So that just leaves us with Claudia and Wesley. And maybe we'll see Wesley tonight, and then…"

"Then we can have a normal visit!"

"That would be very nice," said Luis, and we all clinked glasses.

Mine was a halfhearted clink. I wasn't going to pin my hopes on any hail mary pass in the ninth inning.

Chapter Twenty

Back at home Mickey heard from Dawson that Greta was nowhere to be found. The billiards club only had a cell number for her, and she wasn't answering. Probably because they found the phone stashed in a garbage can in the kitchen.

I called the Bigelows at the hotel, but they didn't answer, so I left a message.

There wasn't much to be done until we were to go to the hospital that night, so Dad suggested that we have an early dinner at 3 Doors Down, one of their favorite haunts. I wasn't too hot on going out, but I insisted to everyone that I was fine and went upstairs to change my clothes.

Mickey was lying on the bed. Dusty was lying next to him, her head resting on his chest while he absentmindedly stroked her back. "Dusty is a lot easier to get along with than Bonkers."

"The two of you look very content. I'm not sure that Mom and Dad allow her up on the bed."

Mickey didn't shift his position. "I won't tell, Dusty won't tell. Our lives are in your hands."

I drew my fingers across my lips, indicating they were zipped shut. "When we get home, I think we should stay in bed for three days and order takeout."

"Sounds good. By the way, I think we should get a bigger place."

"Really? I love the apartment."

"Me, too. But it used to be just for me, and we could use some more room, maybe not right now, but eventually, so I think I'll start looking for places when we get home."

Uh oh, I thought. *He wants room for children.* "That would be exciting."

"Plus, Luis and Ruby need a place to live. Maybe I can find a building that would suit all of us.…"

Great. If we don't have any kids of our own, we can share theirs until we do. "Mickey, um, it's wonderful news about Ruby and the baby, huh?"

He rolled over on his side and regarded me. Dusty sat up and yawned, then jumped down from the bed and sauntered out. "Sure. I'm happy for them."

Pregnant pause, no pun intended.

"So, are you thinking that you and I…?"

He sat up. "Babies? Uh, Annabelle, look, I never thought I would be a good father, and I have to say, if it's really important to you to have children, then we can talk about it, but it's never been something that I felt passionate about, and I'm not confident that…"

He didn't finish because I pounced on him and gave him a huge kiss. "Oh, thank goodness, Mickey. I was worried that you were one of those big family men since you didn't have one yourself."

He smiled. "Neither did you, so I was thinking the same thing about you!"

"We'll be stellar as aunt and uncle to the little Maldonado."

We kissed again. "Do me a favor, babe."

"What?"

"Take off your clothes."

"Mickey, I'm still sore and stiff, and everyone's awake, and these walls aren't very soundproof, and…"

He put a finger to my lips to shush me. "All you'll have to do is lie on your back and be quiet, and all I have to do is kiss you all over."

"All over?" I whispered.

It was all over, not too quickly, and perfectly done.

◇◇◇

The restaurant was convivial, and my parents were greeted like regulars. We all seemed to be ravenous. Dad picked out a wine that we shared while eating hors d'oeuvres of potato fritters dipped in raclette cheese. I could feel our collective tensions give way to lighthearted conversation while we dug into our entrees. Matt the bartender and Zack our waiter kept the glasses filled and the banter flowing. I was starting to feel like I was having a normal visit.

Silly me.

We decided to splurge and have dessert. As our dinner dishes were being cleared away, Dad suddenly bolted up from his chair and pointed out the window. "Is that him?"

We all whipped around to see where he was pointing. A man was standing outside the restaurant and peering in the window. He was short and fat and had blond hair.

Mom put her hand on Dad's arm. "No, dear, it's not. Sit down, now. Take a breath."

We all laughed like this was funny, but the fact was, I had never seen my father so rattled, and it not only upset me, it infuriated me. Jeff Starkey was the best human being the world could ever find, and I couldn't stand that I was once again bringing turmoil into his life.

I excused myself and went to the ladies room. While I was washing my hands, my cell phone rang. I looked at the screen and didn't recognize the number. I hesitated, but dried my hands and answered it.

"Hello?"

"Phil Bigelow here, Anna. Got your message."

"Annabelle. How's Claudia?"

"Just the same. It's hard on Nancy."

But not on you? "Any news about the boyfriend?"

"Nah. He's probably halfway to Syria by now." He guffawed.

"Mr. Bigelow, do you know if Claudia has had any other visitors?"

"Wouldn't know. Why don't we get together again? See if we can hash out some details." He chuckled.

"Will you both be staying in Portland for a while?"

"Well, Nancy's here for the duration. I have a job, after all, so we're driving up to Seattle as we speak. She'll do some laundry, get some more clothes, all of that stuff, then I'll fly to Miami and she'll return here."

"Miami needs a lot of ball bearings, I guess?"

"It's a big business. Hey, I've been meaning to ask you. Are you related to Ringo? Because I never liked the Beatles, but, uh, I could be convinced that I was, uh, mistaken."

Never liked the Beatles? This guy was not only a slimebag, he was a moron.

"Wow, Phil, didn't you figure that out yet? My Dad, he's really Ringo. Look closely next time." He didn't respond. "Thanks for the call. I'll contact Nancy day after tomorrow. Bye."

I hung up before he could say anything else.

I returned to the table and sat down. "I've been slimed." I swallowed some wine. "Phillip Bigelow. Ick. He's going back to Miami to deal with his ball bearings, while his daughter is in a coma. Meanwhile, he talks to me like he's going to ask me out on a date." I took another swallow.

"Well, I certainly hope his balls find their bearings quickly," Mom said brightly.

Everyone laughed but me. Phillip Bigelow had soured my mood and to my mind, the only things to lighten it were the pinot noir and the exquisitely prepared chocolate mousse, into which I dove with my spoon, with abandon.

Chapter Twenty-one

Mickey and I were sitting in Claudia's hospital room, with the dividing curtain drawn so that we couldn't be seen from the doorway. Luis was hanging out in the hospital entrance lobby. None of us knew what Wesley Young looked like, but Luis was going to text us if he saw anyone coming in that could be him. Both Mickey and Luis had gotten on the good side of Dawson and Monroe, apparently. They got the go-ahead to stake out Claudia's room.

Mickey had his gun in his shoulder holster. I assumed Luis was carrying, too. "Mickey, about my gun."

"Mmm. What about it?"

"You know I don't like it."

"You shot pretty well for your first time at the range."

"I'm pretty sure that will be my only time at the range."

"I'm not going to pressure you about this, babe. But I do think we should discuss it some more. Once we're back in New York."

"Okay." I found the remote for the TV and turned it on with the sound muted. "Aha! *Overboard* is on, with Goldie Hawn and Kurt Russell. Ever see it?"

"No. Good?"

"For a light comedy, yup. Goldie Hawn falls off her yacht and has amnesia, and Kurt Russell convinces her that she's his wife and the mother of his four sons. Then she wakes up, but they've fallen in love, so she gives up her upper-crust lifestyle for him and the boys."

"Sorry, it sounds stupid."

"It's good stupid."

"Did you just call me stupid?"

I laughed. "No, I mean it's a good kind of stupid."

Mickey's phone buzzed. He read the text.

"Our Wesley might be entering the building right now."

We both stood up and positioned ourselves toward the head of Claudia's bed and waited.

Sure enough, the door opened and footsteps approached the curtain. A young man in a hoodie pulled it away and bolted out the door as soon as he saw us.

We took off after him. I yelled, "Stop! We just want to talk to you!" but he kept running, and we kept following.

Wesley, assuming it was Wesley, was clearly an athlete. He tore down the hall to the stairwell and flew down the stairs. I tried to keep up, but my body was still recovering from my last run through the woods in stocking feet, so I wasn't up to my usual pace.

Mickey was a step or two behind me, and I figured I was in his way, so I moved over and he raced by me. I continued down, round and round the staircases, ten steps each, then a landing, then ten steps, then a landing.

"Wesley! We want to help!" I yelled. I could hear him still running. Finally I heard a door slam, then open and slam again. I was at the door ready to open it when I heard the shot.

"MICKEY!" I screamed and ran out the door.

Immediately I was tackled to the ground.

"Stay down, Annabelle!" Mickey warned, his body covering mine.

"Are you shot?"

"No. Wesley. He's lying on the ground over there. I don't know where the shooter is. Just stay down." He twisted his body a little to look around, but it was mostly dark; the outside lights of the hospital didn't reach a very far. He reached up to jiggle the door handle, but it had automatically locked when it closed. "Damn it. Babe, we need to get away from the light here and into some dark spot so that we can't be seen."

I nodded, trying to breathe normally.

"Can you crawl?"

"Yup."

"Okay." He pointed. "The corner of the building is just up there. Head straight for it and roll down that little embankment. See it?"

I raised my head to look. "I see it."

"I'm going to run, while you crawl, in case the shooter's there. I'll get his attention."

"Mickey, that doesn't sound like a good idea…"

"No discussion, babe. Ready? On three. One, two, three." Mickey leaped off of me and ran while I crawled. My knees and elbows were not happy, scraping along the cement walkway, but I got to the edge where there was a grassy decline, and I propelled myself over it, rolling down into Mickey's arms.

There were no shots.

Mickey pulled out his phone and speed-dialed Luis. "Side of the building, Luis. Wesley was shot. Can you get to us?" He hung up and moved to squat in front of me. "Stay low, babe. We're okay." Then he called 911 and gave them our location.

Luis came around the building in a crouch. I could make out his silhouette and saw that his gun was drawn. Mickey loud-whispered his name, and Luis scurried down the hill to us. "Are you both all right?"

"Yes," Mickey answered.

"What about Wesley? Is he alive?"

"Don't know. He doesn't seem to be moving." Mickey indicated Wesley's prone body with a nod. "Not even sure it's him, though it's a good bet. We should wait for the police."

"I agree with you. We do not want to be the next targets."

So we sat and waited the few minutes for the police to arrive.

Three squad cars pulled up to the side of the hospital, their headlights blazing across the back expanse. Wesley's body was in full view, stretched out on his stomach like he was ready for a massage.

Mickey and Luis put their guns on the ground and shouted out to the police. One officer came over to us and told us to stay put until it was safe.

I watched two officers approach Wesley. One of them knelt beside him and checked his pulse on the side of his neck. The other cops were fanning out across the parking lot.

Still no shots.

A couple of guys in scrubs brought a gurney. Once the police gave them an all-clear signal, they rolled it up to Wesley and opened up a box that I figured was an EMT's kit.

They bent over Wesley.

Mickey and Luis and I were silent, watching.

They pulled a backboard off the top of the gurney and laid it next to Wesley, quickly sliding it under him. They picked him up and placed him on the gurney and hustled it back into the hospital.

"He's not dead, right? They wouldn't have handled him that way if he was dead, right, Mickey?"

"Right."

I was so relieved I stood up without thinking, and that's when another cop turned his gun on me and yelled "Freeze!"

I threw my hands up in the air, lost my balance, and fell backward down the hill, flashing on Goldie Hawn when she took a tumbler off that yacht.

At least I wasn't going to wake up to mothering four boys. Ever.

Chapter Twenty-two

It was another excruciatingly long night. A million questions, asked and answered, over and over again. At least Dawson and Monroe stood up for us—well, for Mickey and Luis. There was some kind of guy-magic going on there. Monroe still bugged the hell out of me. He had kept sizing me up, trying to stare me down. Little did he know that I was the champion of staring contests. I might be freaking out inside, but I'm not going to look away first, nosiree bob. What did I have to do to stop being regarded as a loose cannon criminal girl from the big city, all about guns and backpacks and putting girls in comas and getting kidnapped by thugs who probably just wanted me to teach them my trick pool shots anyway, and…?

"Babe."

"Huh?"

"You're muttering to yourself."

"Sorry. It's Monroe. He's so irritating." We were alone in the hallway, waiting for Luis.

"He's okay. Just not your style."

"Hmm. I forgot to ask you, Mickey. Did you find out from Monroe and Dawson about us getting stopped twice, and that cop knowing my name?"

"Yeah. The police had your dad's license plate number with your name, just as a if-you-see-this,-keep-an-eye-out sort of thing. Not an APB."

"Oh, that makes me feel SO much better." I rolled my eyes.

Mickey put his arm around me. "Like it or not, you're connected with a murder, and now with Wesley Young getting shot...In fact, I'm reconsidering spending so much time with you myself. Seems very dangerous."

I elbowed him lightly in the ribs.

"Ow! See? You can't be trusted!"

I rolled my eyes again.

Luis walked down the hall toward us and we stood up. "All finished?"

"*Sí, amiga.* These are good police. They are doing a good job."

It was three o'clock in the morning, again, by the time we got back to the house. We came in the front door to find Dusty greeting us and Dad lying on the couch, reading a book. I hadn't called, not wanting to wake him and Mom up. He didn't look happy.

"Dad, we're all okay. I'm sorry I didn't call. There was an, um, incident at the hospital, and we ended up at the police station for the last couple of hours, and..."

"An incident?"

"A shooting, Jeff," Mickey answered. "We were chasing Wesley and someone shot him outside the building. We're fine."

Dad took this in, then stood up and pointed at my face. "You're bleeding?"

"No, Dad. Just scraped. Took a tumble. But I'm great, really!" I hugged him. "Thanks for staying up, though I wish you hadn't. I feel bad that you're not asleep." I let him go.

Dad put his book down on the coffee table. "Bea, Mickey, Luis, this has got to stop. I know that none of this is your fault or your doing, but I can't have Sylvia in danger, and I need to feel confident that Annabelle is as safe as she can be."

"Jeff, I can only say..."

Dad held up his hand to stop Mickey from continuing. "I also know that you will be in other dangerous situations in the future, given your, er, current livelihoods.

"Jeff, I understand that you're worried...."

Dad stopped him again. "My problem is that this young woman here is my extraordinary daughter, my only child. It wasn't that long ago that she had a job as a publicist for a publishing company in San Francisco, and now she's chasing bad guys, getting kidnapped, and being harmed. I don't like it."

None of us said anything.

"But how she leads her life, and how the two of you lead yours, is all up to you. I ask for only one thing."

"Name it, please, Dad. You're freaking me out with all of this serious father talk. I feel like it's 1999 when I was seventeen and stayed out on New Year's Eve partying like it was 1999, remember that song?, and I came home at two, and you were so pissed off at me I thought I would be grounded in solitary confinement until George Clooney actually got married, which would have been right around now, come to think of it, and that would make it, like, fifteen years in solitary, and..."

"Beatrice Annabelle Starkey, please shut up."

I did.

"Here are my conditions. You must give me all the details, all the time. I cannot sit here and wonder if you are in trouble. You must figure out ways to call if something goes wrong. And you must let me and Sylvia help, however we can. We're in this, too, now."

This was not what I was expecting to hear. I thought Dad was going to ask Mickey to take me back to New York. "Oh, Dad, jeez, of course. We won't put you through this again, I promise." I kissed his cheek. "Let's all go to bed."

"Mickey? Luis?"

"I hear you loud and clear, sir," said Luis.

"Jeff, again, I can't apologize enough, and yes, we will keep you posted on all the details while we're here."

"Fair enough." Dad picked up his book. "I'm going to bed. Sleep well." He left us.

Mickey and I said goodnight to Luis, walked into the guest room, and shut the door. "Your old man," Mickey said, "is not like anyone I've ever met."

"Solid, through and through. We can't worry him anymore. I'm glad Mom went to bed, anyway." I kicked off my shoes. "I wonder if we'll ever have a normal visit with them?"

Mickey flopped on the bed. "We will. We'll invite them to New York, sometime when we don't have any cases, and we'll do touristy things."

"Until then, Mickey…will we find out anything about Wesley tomorrow, do you think?"

"Hope so. Maybe they'll even have found the shooter by now. They had a lot of officers combing the area after we left."

"Maybe you and I will solve this mystery without the police. Like Luther and Alice Morgan, only you're not a cop any longer and I'm not a psychopath."

Mickey yawned. "What in God's name are you talking about?"

I planted my palms on the sides of my face. "Luther? You never watched *Luther*? BBC series starring Idris Elba? Jeez, Mickey. As soon as I think you're a highly educated man, you stun me with something like this. I'll have to have to reconsider our entire relationship."

He pulled me onto the bed and gave me a long kiss. "Enough reconsidering?" he mumbled.

"Yup."

We went to sleep.

Chapter Twenty-three

Just when we thought things were getting clearer, the case got muddier than a pig sty. While we didn't know what the hell Loren Scranton was up to, we saw no connection between him and Claudia. We assumed that Wesley Young was recovering in the hospital from a gunshot wound, while whoever shot him would soon be arrested. We assumed Claudia would eventually wake up (well, I assumed that anyway, putting on my best Pollyanna mindset), and we assumed that Greta and Julius were connected to all of it, theorizing that the gun that killed Hank Howard or Howard Hanks came from them, or else why would they have kidnapped me?

But, like I said, things got as crystal clear as a brick wall.

The first wrong assumption had to do with Wesley Young. It turned out that the guy we chased out of the hospital wasn't Wesley Young at all. He had no ID on him, but once he started talking to the police, he said he was a friend of Wesley's and was looking in on Claudia for him.

His name was Ricky Martin, and I'm not kidding.

When the police asked him who he thought might have shot him, he said he didn't have a clue.

Dawson told Mickey he didn't believe anything Ricky said.

The shooter seemed to have gotten away from the police as fast as a pop-up fly ball.

The next assumption that was wholly mistaken was that Loren Scranton was a separate matter. We were astonished to hear that he had visited Claudia in the hospital, according to a nurse—who wasn't Tiffany.

"*Huh*?" I wondered aloud, when Mickey was giving us the recap he got from Dawson on the phone. We crowded around the dining room table, drinking coffee and eating cheesy scrambies, prepared by Mickey. "Scranton *is* involved in this mess after all? Are you serious?"

Mickey sighed. "He might have gone to the hospital as part of his stalking routine. Maybe he followed you and Sylvia there, but didn't get to Claudia's room until you had left."

Mom took a swig of coffee. "That's possible. We weren't in the room very long, and then we went to the cafeteria. That prickbrain."

"Well," said Dad, "if he shows up again we'll put a restraining order on him. I wonder how long he'll be in Portland?"

No one answered, since no one knew.

"Okay, so what are we doing today?" Dad continued.

"I still think we should try to find Wesley Young. He could be the answer to many questions," replied Luis.

"I agree," said Mickey, "even though the police are probably conducting their own search. Annabelle, when were the Bigelows going to be back in town?"

"Mr. B was going to Miami. Mrs. B should be back today. Let's go see her."

Mom stood up. "Sounds like a plan. I'll do the dishes while you all get showered and dressed."

Mickey, Luis, and I traded glances. "Um, Mom, I don't think all five of us should go. I think you and Dad should stay here."

Dad regarded me over the top of his glasses. "Nancy Bigelow might open up to your mother, a doctor and a mother herself."

I couldn't believe that Dad was suggesting that Mom play detective, given everything that had transpired over the last couple of days, even given the previous night's conversation. "I don't want to overwhelm her, is all," I sputtered.

Luis stood up. "I do not have to go, Annabelle. Your mother could be an asset. I think you are right, Jeff. I will see if I can dig up any information on Greta and her friend Julius. Perhaps there will be some lead as to who was with Julius when he kidnapped you."

I was about to protest again when Mickey stopped me. "It's fine for Sylvia to come, and thank you, Sylvia, for helping. You, too, Jeff."

Dad turned his attention to the newspaper. "You see Scranton, you know what to do."

"Are you talking to me, dear, because I know exactly what I'm going to do to that sleazy snake if he shows up." Mom turned on the faucet in the sink.

"I wasn't talking to you, Syl."

"We just want you to talk to Nancy Bigelow, Mom, okay? No shenanigans."

Mom laughed. "Yes, boss."

But we didn't end up going to see Nancy Bigelow, because one of my assumptions was correct: Claudia Bigelow woke up.

◇◇◇

We were back at the hospital—Mom, Mickey, and me. We heard the news about Claudia because when I called Nancy on her cell phone, she was already at Claudia's bedside. Claudia had woken up in the very wee hours of the morning, and Nancy had raced down from Seattle. I asked her if it would be okay for us to stop by. She told me the police had come and gone, and that Claudia was very tired, but that she already told Nancy that she wanted to see me. She remembered that she had set up a meeting, and that she was attacked.

When we walked into the room, Claudia was propped up in bed, sipping through a straw. Nancy was seated by the window, casually leafing through a *People* magazine. It was a really old one, with Jennifer Lopez and her kids on the cover. She was so good in that 1990s movie with George Clooney, *Out of Sight*. Since then, well, no comment.

Anyway, Nancy greeted us, then pointed at her daughter. "She's back!"

Claudia put her cup down and smoothed out the sheets in front of her. She looked exhausted.

Mom walked around to the far side of the bed and took Claudia's hand. "How are you feeling, dear? I'm the doctor who found you at the Japanese Garden."

Claudia half smiled. "I'm doing all right. I have a headache, and I'm really tired." She sized up me and Mickey. "Are you the detective?"

Mickey nodded. "Yes, I'm…"

"No, I meant you," she interrupted, pointing at me.

"I'm Annabelle Starkey, yes, the person you called. You ended up with my backpack. This is Mickey, my partner."

"Glad to see you awake," Mickey said.

Claudia kept her eyes on me. "The police told me that you *did* have the backpack with the gun."

"Yes."

"You didn't tell me that when I called."

"No."

"Why not?"

"You said you were in trouble. I wanted to see if I could help, and I wanted to find out why I ended up with that gun." I approached her on the opposite side of the bed from Mom. "Do you still need my help?"

Claudia pulled her hand away from Mom and folded her arms across her chest. "I don't know."

"Claudia, what about Wesley Young?" asked Mickey. "Were you getting the gun for him, or from him, for some reason?"

Claudia clenched her teeth. "Wesley has nothing to do with this."

Nancy stood up abruptly. "That's what you keep saying, but we don't believe you. He was never any good for you. He hit you once, remember? My God, Claudia, you can't keep protecting a criminal!" She leaned on the foot of the bed. "Tell these people what you told the police."

"Wesley didn't hit me and I didn't tell the police anything."

"Exactly my point! How can we help you if you won't talk to us? You know as soon as you feel better the police will probably arrest you."

"For what, Mom? For getting mugged? For saying that the backpack was supposed to be for me? I haven't broken any laws."

Mickey sighed. "She's right. They can hold her for questioning, I suppose, but they have no proof that the gun was supposed to be hers, other than Annabelle telling them so."

Claudia glared at me. "Thanks for that, by the way."

"Hey! We probably saved your life, little missy, so I'd can the Lindsay Lohan whiny act, if I were you! You asked for my help, remember? And police show up when someone gets beaned on a hillside in the middle of the day!"

Mickey put his hand on my arm to stop me.

Claudia started crying. Mom pulled a tissue out of the box by the bed and gave it to her.

Nancy sat back down. "Here we go again. Darling daughter, we all know that you're in some kind of trouble, but we can't help you if you don't tell us what's going on."

"I don't know who mugged me, okay?!" Claudia shouted. "And I'm not going to talk to you about why I wanted that gun!" She was still shouting.

Mickey and I traded a quick look. *Aha. She at least admitted that the gun was hers.*

Nancy gulped, stunned. "What? You have to tell the police."

"I'll deny I said anything about that if any of you tell them."

Mom patted the top of her head. "Calm down now. We don't have to go over all of this right now. But I would like to ask you how you know Loren Scranton."

"Who?"

"Loren Scranton."

"Don't know him."

"He came to visit you."

"Must have been asleep."

"What about the note, Claudia?" I stepped in.

"What note?"

"The one I found in your drawer. It's gone now. Someone took it. But wait, here's a picture of it." I pulled out my phone, dialed it up, and held the screen in front of her face.

Now, she didn't look so hot anyway, but when she read that note, her complexion grayed to the hue of Richard Gere's hair. She tried to fake it, though. "I don't know what that is. I have never seen it before."

I knew she was lying. Her bluff was as transparent as Jennifer Lopez's clothes.

With that, she reached over to the buttons to level the bed and announced that she needed to rest and would everyone please leave. Nancy didn't move, but Claudia said, "You, too, Mom." Nancy threw the magazine on the floor and huffed out, saying she might as well go back to the hotel and get some rest.

Mom told Claudia to rest and that we were her friends, then Mickey followed Mom out the door. I lingered for a few seconds, waiting for them to be out, and keeping my eyes on Claudia's face.

I wasn't completely surprised when she whispered, "Come back. Alone."

I nodded and left.

Beatrice Annabelle Starkey, DDS, was about to be hired on her first case as a detective. Not Mickey, not Luis. Nope, me. I'm the one the client wanted.

Holy crap.

Chapter Twenty-four

I saw Nancy outside before I got in the car. When I asked her if Phillip would be returning to Portland from Miami sooner than planned, since Claudia was awake, she said he was rearranging his schedule and would be in Portland later or the next morning. I also said it was smart for her to go back to the hotel.

She looked at me suspiciously. "Why do you say that?"

"To be perfectly frank," I lied, "you look completely worn out. I'm just hoping you'll be able to get some solid sleep." I plastered what I hoped was a caring smile on my face. I couldn't believe this woman was going to leave her daughter's bedside at this point.

"Well, that's very nice of you," she too-sweetly responded, "but don't you worry about me. And don't bother Claudia anymore. I don't want her stress to compound while she's in the hospital. We need to give her some time to regain her strength."

"I'm sure you're right. She's lucky to have you in her corner," I lied again. "By the way, I think you know all about Greta from the Uptown Billiards Club. The working theory is that it was her gun that was on its way to Claudia, and it was her gun that murdered her ex-boyfriend."

"Yes, yes, the police have told me."

"Well, I want to make sure you understand that your daughter could still be in danger."

"Well, of course I understand that!" She fumbled with her car keys. "I really must go now." She rushed off.

After we got in the car I told Mickey and Mom what Claudia had said to me. I also told them about my conversation with Nancy.

Mickey sighed and rubbed his face.

"What, Mickey?"

"Nothing. Just too much information, maybe. You don't know that the police already told her all of that about Greta. It's better to keep the information we have to ourselves until we know more."

"I think she knew, Mickey." But I wasn't sure. Mickey was right. Me and my big mouth again.

Mom drove while Mickey called Luis from the car to let him know about Claudia and to find out if there was any progress made on Wesley Young and his friend Ricky. Apparently there was, based on the amount of time Mickey was silent, listening to Luis. We were exiting the parking lot when Mickey hung up.

"What happened?" I asked.

"Luis called your friend Perry at that bar, the Rowdy something?"

"Yeats."

"Right. Clint meets William Butler. Anyway, he asked him about Ricky, gave a description, told him it was in relation to Hank Howard. Perry seems to think he's seen Ricky around, so your Dad and Luis are on their way over there to show him Ricky's picture."

"We have Ricky's picture?" Mom asked.

"Luis found him on Facebook. Printed his photo."

"Are you sure he didn't find the wrong Ricky Martin?"

Mickey chuckled. "Yeah. This Ricky is twenty-four years old and lives in Seattle. And he's friends with someone who's friends with Claudia."

"Let's go to The Rowdy Yeats. I like Perry, and I feel like playing pool again."

"If it's okay with Sylvia, it's okay with me, Fats."

"Don't call me that ever again."

◇◇◇

Dad and Luis were already at the bar when we arrived, beers in hand. Perry was peering at the photo of Ricky. He looked up when we approached. "Just heard about your trouble at the hospital. Glad you're okay."

I smiled. "Thanks."

"Beers?"

Mom nodded. Mickey held up three fingers.

"Oh, Perry, this is Mickey Paxton. He's partners with me and Luis."

Perry held his hand out across the bar and Mickey shook it.

"And this is my mother, Sylvia Starkey."

Perry shook her hand, too. "Pleasure."

"All mine, Perry."

Introductions made and beers supplied, Perry focused on the picture again. "I'm pretty sure this is the guy I saw in here a week or two ago, and he definitely was with another guy. You're thinking it could have been this Wesley Young dude?"

Every time someone said Wesley Young's name I thought about Wesley Snipes, the actor. I mean, how many Wesleys can one know about in one lifetime? And whenever I flashed on Wesley Snipes, I thought about the movie *Brooklyn's Finest,* when he played a bad guy trying to be good, and I had to stop myself from imagining that our Wesley was in the same predicament.

Luis asked Perry if he could describe Wesley, and if he could remember anything the two friends talked about when they were at the bar. Perry leaned against the back counter. "I can tell you this. The other guy, not Ricky, was nervous. Slugged down three shots of tequila in short order. Was fidgety. They didn't stay long." Perry looked at the floor for a moment, then snapped his fingers. "They paid with a credit card. You want the number? I can find the receipt."

"That would be very helpful, thank you," said Luis. Mom followed with, "Now we're fucking getting somewhere."

That made Perry do a double take, but he went in the back room to find the receipt.

No one was playing pool, so I slid quarters into the table slot, chalking my cue stick while the balls rolled into view. I set them up in the triangle and positioned the cue ball to break.

Kablam.

Damn, I love that sound.

The ten-ball dropped in the far corner, while the fourteen fell in a side pocket. "Whoo hoo! I'm stripes! Who wants solids?"

Dad, Mom, Luis, and Mickey were all on stools, backs to the bar, beer bottles in hand, watching me. Mickey leaned over and said to Dad, "Tough kid you've got there." They clinked bottles. Dad was about to stand up to play, but Mom beat him to it. "Who do you think taught her?" She winked at Mickey.

Yup. I was screwed. Mom is the real shark in the family.

She picked out a cue stick just as Perry came tearing out of the back room. "Outside!" he yelled.

"You want us to leave?" Mickey stood up and faced him.

"Look outside!"

We all rushed to the window. "See that guy, across the street? He's the one who was in here with Ricky!"

I was out of the door in a flash, with Mickey and Luis close behind me. I heard Dad say, "No, Sylvia, let them do this. You stay here with me."

Wesley—at least we hoped it was Wesley—saw us tearing down the sidewalk at him, and he did what any sane person would do in that situation. He ran.

My feet didn't hurt so much anymore, and I had on my running shoes instead of my new cowboy boots, so I was gaining on him, ahead of my *compadres*.

I finally got close enough to take him down.

With my pool stick.

I tossed it like a javelin—I guess, though I've never thrown a javelin in my life—and its point hit him in the small of his back. It wasn't hard, but it surprised him and he lost his balance and fell. I pulled up next to him, panting, and Mickey grabbed him when he started to clamber to his feet.

"Are you Snipes?" I yelled at him.

Mickey and Luis looked confused.

Wesley did, too. "What? No! I'm Wesley Young!"

"Right. That's what I meant."

Mickey shook his head and he and Luis led Wesley back to The Rowdy Yeats. I picked up my pool cue, dusted it off against my jeans, and blew on its tip, for good luck.

"Please don't call the police, please!" Wesley begged us. We were all gathered in the back room at The Rowdy Yeats, courtesy of Perry, who remained at the bar, serving his customers and probably trying to act like it was a normal to have a pile of detectives and parents and a wanted man hashing it out on one's premises. We had gone over everything with Wesley, including Ricky getting shot and about me being kidnapped. He had not been cooperating.

"Maybe we won't call the police," said Mickey, straddling a chair and looking so macho and cool that I was having a hard time taking my eyes off of him. "That will all depend on the answers you give us. Stalling will only increase our desire to bring the police in on this. So, shall we start over?"

Wesley nodded reluctantly.

"Okay, then. Did you kill Howard Hanks?"

"NO! I don't even know someone by that name!"

"How about Hank Howard?" I asked.

"No!"

"Next question," Mickey continued. "Do you know Loren Scranton?"

"No."

"What about Greta and Julius at the Uptown Billiards Club?"

Pause. "I've been there."

"And?"

"That's all. I went with Ricky. Drinks and pool. He might know them. I think he goes there a lot."

"Why were you afraid to visit Claudia last night?" I was tossing the pool cue back and forth between my hands.

"What? I wasn't afraid. I've been seeing her every night!"

"Ricky said he checked up on her because you asked him to."

Pause. "No shit. Wow. I didn't send him. I told him I was careful when I visited. I didn't want to be there when her mother and father were around. They don't like me."

"I should say not. You hit their daughter."

Wesley started to spring out of his chair but Luis was standing behind him and pushed him back down. "I never hit Claudia! Ever! Mrs. Bigelow is crazy and she's making Claudia crazy."

"Well, they say you punched her, and I suppose she was exhibiting some evidence to that effect."

Wesley looked bewildered and panicky. "When? She never told me she was hit."

"The Bigelows say you hit her."

"I DIDN'T!"

Mickey took over. "How did you find out she had been mugged and was in a coma? Did you follow her there?"

Pause. "Okay. I did know she was going to the garden. She posted a picture of it on Instagram. I texted her that I'd find her there, but she told me not to come and that she'd meet me later. I decided to go there anyway to make sure she was all right, because she'd been acting all jumpy the last few days. When I got there the ambulance had already arrived. I saw them putting her in the back."

"That's pretty lame, Wesley," Mom jeered. I don't think anyone here believes you."

I thought, *Well, I sort of do believe him, and are my parents really partners in Asta Investigations now, or should I suggest that they leave?*

"Why did Claudia need a gun?" Luis asked.

"I didn't know she needed a gun. Honestly, like I said, she had been acting a little cagey, that's why I showed up at the garden. She didn't tell me anything about a gun." Wesley turned his head around to Mom. "I'm not lying, ma'am."

I walked to his side to block his view of my mother. "Had you planned to get together in Portland? You both were meeting in secret, away from Seattle?"

"Yes. Like I said, her parents don't like me."

"One more question." I squatted down next to him, the pool cue upright on the floor providing a prop for balance. "Why would someone shoot Ricky? Who would shoot Ricky? Do you think whoever it was thought Ricky was you?"

"That's three questions."

Luis flicked Wesley's head. "Watch it, *idiota*. Answer the *senorita*."

"I don't know, any of it."

Mickey stood up. "We have to call the police, Wesley. They're investigating Claudia's attack, and they've been looking for you. If it makes a difference, I believe you."

"You *do*?" Mom was incredulous. "I think this kid is a lying loser!"

I held my finger to my lips to quiet her and was about to say something when Wesley cut me off. "About Ricky." We waited. "You told me about being kidnapped?" I nodded. "He drives a van sometimes."

"Dark green?" I asked.

"Yes."

"He's a good pal of yours, this Ricky?" Dad ventured.

Wesley shook his head. "Not anymore."

"That's the smartest thing you've said all afternoon," commented Mom, while Mickey pulled out his phone to call the police.

Chapter Twenty-five

"Mickey, what are we going to do about my parents?" I was sitting with him on the back porch, speaking quietly.

"What do you mean?"

"I don't want them to be our partners."

He laughed. "I think Jeff is involved mostly to look after Sylvia, who seems very invested in solving everything as fast as possible. But I doubt they want to start up the West Coast office of Asta Investigations."

"Oh, don't even joke about that!"

"It will all be over soon. Wesley's with the police, maybe they'll find the van since Ricky's still in the hospital. He'll have to come clean, I think, since Wesley basically ratted him out. It must have been Ricky who was with Julius."

I shrugged. "Seems like the most likely explanation, though I didn't recognize him when he came to the hospital room. But he ran out of there so fast. Actually, I didn't get a good look at him when I kicked him in the face at the back of the van, either."

He put his arm around me and pulled me close. "I've always said you have great legs. Look, we still don't know why Claudia wanted that gun, but I bet the police can get more information out of both Ricky and Wesley, and even Claudia. She's young. She'll get scared and spill the beans."

I didn't respond.

"Babe?"

"Claudia wants to spill the beans to me. I want to go back to the hospital tonight."

"Okay. Luis and I will go with you."

I pulled away from him. "No, Mickey. She was clear. She wants to talk to me alone. She'll clam up if you guys are there. This is a girl thing."

"You don't know that."

"Yup, I think I do. For some reason she thinks she can trust me, and it's probably because I agreed to meet her, and because I'm female. Look, we can handle this like before, only this time both you and Luis will be outside in the car. That way you can keep an eye out for any other visitors while I'm inside."

"Okay."

"I just have one other condition."

He brushed the hair from my face and kissed my cheek. "Mmm. What."

"You don't bring Mom or Dad with you."

He kissed my other cheek. "Deal."

We went inside. Luis was on the front porch talking to Ruby. Mom and Dad had gone over to Sal and Drew's. "How shall we kill some time?" Mickey's eyes twinkled.

I faked a yawn. "Damn, I'm super tired. Nap?"

We raced each other up the stairs.

After Mickey and I, um, "woke up," we found Luis and Mom and Dad gathered around the coffee table, perusing some more restaurant supply catalogs. Luis was pointing to a picture, saying, "I like this one very much."

The things you find out about people. Luis? An interior decorator?

I nudged him over on the couch and took a look.

It wasn't a restaurant supply catalog after all.

It was a handgun catalog, and he was pointing at a Smith & Wesson .357 Magnum, clearly identified in bold type.

"What the hell!" I bolted upright, darting my eyes from my mother to my father and back again.

"Easy, muffinhead. We're just investigating, learning a little about firearms. Maybe for home protection. Maybe for the bakery."

Mickey squatted by the coffee table and peered at the open pages. "Not a bad idea, and I agree with Luis, that one would do the trick."

"THE TRICK? SHOOTING SOMEONE IS A TRICK?" I howled.

Luis tugged on my arm and brought me back to sitting on the couch. "*Amiga*, why are you so upset? Mickey has a gun. I have a gun. You even have a gun. Your parents, they are thinking about it. That is all."

I made my voice calm. "My parents have never liked guns and have never wanted a gun in their house." I leaned over and shut the catalog. "This is all because of us, because of me, right? You're scared now, of home invasions? Because I got kidnapped? Have you forgotten that there were *two* guns in the house when I was kidnapped, and they didn't offer any protection at that moment? Did you also forget that if you had just LOCKED YOUR DOOR slimebag Scranton wouldn't have waltzed in here to leave his goddam calling card?"

"Babe..."

I held my palm flat out toward Mickey. "No, I'm not finished. It's one thing for you and Luis to carry guns. You're police, ex-police. You're highly trained. It's entirely different for my parents to become vigilantes. All of you know that accidents with guns happen because *people have guns in their houses*! No guns, no accidental shootings!" I flopped backward on the couch. "What the hell?"

"Darling, we haven't decided to buy a gun. Sal and Drew had this catalog..."

"Mom, what? They have guns, Sal and Drew?"

"Gay people shoot, too, sweetheart."

"That's not what I meant. I just, well..." I stopped because I realized it *was* what I meant. I couldn't imagine Sal and Drew or any gay men that I knew wanting to own a gun. And I couldn't think of any movies where the cops or the good guys were gay and shooting guns. I couldn't think of any gun-toting bakers, either. Of course, gay men would have plenty of reasons to own guns, what with homophobic maniacs running around convinced that homosexuals are out to ruin civilization. So call me a stereotyper. But Sal and Drew?

"They have guns?" I repeated.

Luis jumped in. "I understand Annabelle's concern. When we leave here, you will not have the disturbing events of this week continuing. We will have resolved them. You should lock your doors, put an alarm on your bakery, and leave it at that. And," he smiled at Mom, "you have your own built-in firepower, Sylvia. I have seen it and heard it myself. You are very strong, and you have your fine husband here who is also very strong."

"And an arsenal right across the street!" I added.

Dad chuckled. "An arsenal of flour, muffin. I think they have just one gun, not a closetful."

I flashed on the scene in *Witness* when Harrison Ford hides his bullets in the flour tin at the Amish family's house, so the little boy won't end up playing with a loaded gun.

And I thought, *Who knows what's in that kitchen across the street from my precious parents?*

Mickey stood up. "I'll toss my hat into the no-gun-for-the-Starkeys ring. My guess is you'll never be involved in a violent episode again in your lives."

How I wished that to be so. But wishes are as reliable as movie reviews posted on Yelp by sixteen-year-olds who love Justin Bieber.

I begged for the Brussels sprouts pizza for dinner, so Dad picked it up along with a more conservative pepperoni model. I made a salad, and we all munched comfortably on our food while gathered in the den in front of *The Graduate*. Mom and Dad had it on DVD, and Luis, I remembered, had never seen it. Near the end, in the church scene, Mom and I hammed it up, yelling "Elaine!" along with Dustin Hoffman in our most pleading voices, until Dad joined us by yelling "Ben!" with Katharine Ross. Then we howled with laughter while Mickey and Luis tolerated our silliness with bemused looks. It felt good to let off some steam.

Before we left for the hospital, I was gathering my hat and gloves from the bedroom when I saw the rabbit chopsticks I had purchased at the Japanese Garden. I picked one up and rubbed it between my fingers. Nice and smooth, lacquered wood. The tip was not sharp, but it was pointier than other chopsticks I had seen. The little rabbits painted on the ends were white and sweet as could be. I wondered about their symbolism. Then I thought about how they are said to proliferate quickly and abundantly.

Maybe these were the wrong chopsticks for Mickey and me.

My hair was long enough to twist on top of my head, so I used two of the chopsticks to hold it in place, feeling a little silly but a little pretty, too. I had to add some bobby pins to secure my 'do, but after inspecting my handiwork in a mirror, I decided it wasn't half bad for someone who usually solves hairdo issues by wearing hats.

My sock-monkey hat wouldn't fit over this new head of mine, so I dropped it on the bed and trotted downstairs.

Mickey did a double take when he saw me. "Cute. The sticks are kind of long, aren't they?"

I scrunched up my nose. "Shall I trade them for the sock monkey?"

"Please don't. Absolutely not. You look fantastic, I mean it, really."

Luis was waiting for us outside. As Mickey and I headed out, I cautioned my parents. "Lock the door."

Mom rolled her eyes. "You are such a pain in the ass," she said, right before she shut it.

And locked it.

Chapter Twenty-six

When Mickey brought Dad's car to a stop in front of the hospital, I got out, and he did, too.

"Mickey, we agreed. I go in alone."

"I could wait in the hall."

"I don't want Claudia to see you. What if she wants to go for a walk in the hall with me, just to move around a bit?"

"Okay." He kissed me. "Be careful."

It was about nine o'clock, and the hospital was pretty quiet. I took the elevator up to Claudia's room and entered.

She was sitting up, watching a *Modern Family* rerun. "I bet Cameron and Mitchell don't have guns," I ventured.

She jerked her head around to see me. "Close the door, will you?"

I did and took a seat on the ledge by the window, dangling my feet. "How are you feeling?"

"Better. I think they're going to let me out tomorrow."

"Wow. Fast."

"No more headache."

I fiddled with my Japanese hairdo. "So, what do you want to tell me?"

Claudia fidgeted with her sheets and fixed her eyes on the television. I reached over to the remote and shut it off. "I like this show, too, but I didn't come here to watch TV with you." I set the remote on the ledge next to me, beyond her reach.

"Look, you have to believe me that Wesley had nothing to do with any of this."

"Okay. The police are sorting that out with him."

"The police?! They arrested him? Oh shit!" She started crying.

I took a tissue out of the box and handed it to her. "They are at least questioning him. I don't think they've arrested him. They're also questioning Ricky Martin, who is still in this hospital somewhere with a bullet wound. And it turns out, as I'm sure you know, that Ricky and Wesley are friends. Or at least used to be. And, missy, it's also looking like Ricky was involved in kidnapping me. So I really think it's time you filled me in, pronto-like. *Comprende?*"

I think using Spanish words makes me sound tougher, no offense to Latinos.

Claudia blew her nose and lay back on her pillows. "Ricky got the gun for me."

"Why?"

"For protection."

"From whom?"

"Can't tell you that. But it's not Wesley!"

"Who hit you? Your parents said someone hit you, and they're sure it was Wesley."

"No one hit me."

"Okkaaayyyy. So why do you think you were mugged? Was it Ricky? Did he think you still had the gun and he wanted it back?"

Claudia nodded. "That's all I can figure."

"How would he have found you in the Japanese Garden, if Wesley hadn't told him you were there?"

She looked up at the ceiling to avoid my eyes. "I don't know. Maybe it wasn't Ricky who mugged me."

"Is he your friend, really?"

"I only know him a little bit. I heard him talking to Wesley once about some people he hangs with, and he said something about a gun, so I found his number on Wesley's phone and I texted him. That's how it happened."

"Why would he come here to visit you?"

"I DON'T KNOW," she shouted at me. "Maybe he thinks I still have the gun, or I'm going to turn him in to the police, or something. Maybe he wants to kill me! Fuck!"

I stood up and started pacing back and forth alongside her bed, giving her some time to calm down. "So when you called me, why did you ask for my help? The help of a detective? You still thought I had your gun, and that's all you wanted, right?"

"You said you didn't have it. I was supposed to get rid of it after I, uh, once I didn't need it anymore. I didn't know if you were lying or not, but I didn't want that gun to be anywhere other than the bottom of the river if it wasn't with me. I was scared, and I thought I needed you to find the gun, if you didn't already have it."

I sat back down on the ledge. "Claudia, I have to tell you, this is all sounding really stupid. You put yourself in danger, just because you decided you needed a gun, for reasons you won't tell me. And you still won't tell me who you're afraid of. How can my partners and I protect you?" I paused and stared at her, but she didn't respond. "Is it Loren Scranton?"

"I told you, I don't know him."

"He came to visit you!"

She frowned. "Like I said before, I don't remember any stranger coming in here."

I shrugged. "Okay, it was probably when you were still unconscious. Are you sure you don't know him?"

"Positive."

I blew some air out through my pursed lips. "So, what do you want from me now?"

Claudia sat up straight. "I want you to protect Wesley, and that's it. The whole gun thing is over as far as I'm concerned."

"That's probably a good thing, but does that mean you no longer think you're in danger?"

She slumped. "I'll be all right."

"You're driving me crazy, you know that? I can't protect Wesley without more information."

"I don't have any more information to give you."

The door opened suddenly and I heard a low voice say, "That's a good girl. Keep your fucking mouth shut."

I turned and saw Julius, big and ugly and scary-looking. So I did what any brave detective would do in a similar situation. I screamed bloody murder, louder than Janet Leigh in *Psycho*, and ran at him with every ounce of strength I had.

He maybe budged an inch, if that.

He grabbed my arm and covered my mouth with his other hand. "Shut the fuck up."

Then he pulled out a gun and pointed it at Claudia.

She was a quick learner. Her scream was even louder than mine.

I watched her roll out of the bed onto the floor on its far side.

I was squirming around as much as I could. Julius' hands were monstrous, but they were fleshy. I managed to open my mouth a little and clamp my teeth down on his palm, behind his thumb.

"SHIT!" he yelled.

His hand came off my mouth. I kicked his shin and turned away from him while grabbing a chopstick from my hair. I rammed it as hard as I could into his cheek. The one on his face, I mean.

"FUCK!" he howled, and let me go.

I ran out into the hall, screaming for someone to call the police. I saw a couple of nurses dashing toward Claudia's room, having already heard the commotion. "He has a gun! Don't go in, just call 911!" I warned them. They came to a dead stop, turned around, and rushed to the nurses' station to call.

I didn't want to leave Claudia in there, helpless, on the floor. My phone was in my purse on the window ledge, so I couldn't call Mickey or Luis. I peered around the door and saw Julius moving toward Claudia, gun in hand.

I dove and landed on his back. He fell to his knees and dropped the gun. It skittered away from him. I shouted to Claudia. "Get out of here now, Claudia!" She scurried out from under the bed and into the hallway.

Julius was trying to stand up again. I was flailing away at him like the worst monkey on his back he'd ever known, hitting at his face, his head, his neck, anything I could hit.

Like I intimated earlier, he was bigger than Bigfoot, and no, I don't believe in Sasquatch, but there I was in the Pacific Northwest and it occurred to me that Julius could be a shaved version. Mostly shaved, anyway.

He quickly was able to throw me off and I landed hard on my side.

We heard people running down the hall. He snarled at me, picked up his gun, and threw me over his shoulder like a sack of potatoes. He walked out of the room, pointing his gun at the security guards hustling toward us. "Stop right there, or I put a bullet in her head, and then all of you are next."

I kept pounding on him, but I was running out of steam.

His gun was pressed against my side. "Stop moving, or I'll plant a bullet in your uterus instead."

What a pig.

But I stopped.

Nimble for a monster, Julius descended the same stairs where Ricky had run, and hurried out the back door. I was hanging onto the back of his shirt to keep from swaying from side to side like a pendulum.

I figured this was it. He'd kill me in the parking lot.

Then I came to my senses and my fear left me quicker than a bullet leaves a gun, as Tom Waits once wrote in a song.

Out of the corner of my eye I saw Luis, gun drawn, and I heard Mickey approach behind us. "Let her go, now, or you're dead," he commanded.

Julius stopped. Luis came up in front of him with his gun aimed at his head, while Mickey closed in from behind. He stuck his gun in Julius' back. "Now."

Julius loosened his grip. I slid to the ground, panting. Luis took Julius' gun away from him. Mickey with his gun persuaded Julius to sit.

"You all right, Annabelle?"

"Peachy, Mickey."

"Where's your purse?"

"Huh?"

"You know, dental floss? You always carry it? I'd love to tie up this dirtbag right now."

I smiled. "Aw, you're heading down memory lane now, aren't you sweetie? Sorry, my purse is upstairs in Claudia's room."

"This is not a problem." Luis extracted some plastic zip-ties from his pocket and went to work on Julius' hands and feet while Mickey kept his gun on him.

"His face is bleeding, babe. You do that?"

"Chopstick. We probably won't want to eat with that one in the future."

"Too bad. It was a nice idea, you buying those for us."

"Thanks, sweetheart." I was sitting on the ground, thinking that this conversation was one of the most surreal of my life.

Mickey and Luis situated Julius against the side of the building. Luis kept him covered with his gun, while Mickey came over and sat down beside me on the ground. "Tell me something good."

"I'm glad you came with me tonight." I started trembling.

"Me, too." He rubbed my arms and drew me close. "I think we should get married."

I laughed. "Really? That's your proposal? Right here, right now, in the parking lot sitting next to a bloody oversized disgusting excuse for a human being?"

"You want me to kneel?"

I hugged him. "No, I want you to marry me."

Chapter Twenty-seven

The police sorted it out. Julius, the Neanderthal, sang like a canary on speed. He not only confessed to shooting at Ricky as well as kidnapping me, he said he did all of it on orders from Greta, and that Greta killed Howard. Or Hanks. Whatever.

The gun was hers. Apparently she didn't like it that Hanks was going straight and was trying to get her to do the same, to the point that he threatened to call the cops on her. She did a bit of dealing when she wasn't bartending.

Ricky worked for Greta, delivering drugs. When Claudia called him about getting a gun, he asked Greta if she could supply one, and she gave it to him. Maybe she was trying to set Ricky up. Maybe she figured the police would never connect her with Hanks. Anyway, Ricky left it in the backpack at the airport. When we met Greta and told her that I ended up with the gun, she called Julius and told him to follow us and get the gun from me. He followed us to my parents' house, then came back later with Ricky in the van. They had some harebrained idea that they'd hold me for ransom for the gun, and some dough on the side for good measure.

Wesley continued to profess complete ignorance about all of it, insisting that he was as innocent as a Virgin Mary, and I guess he meant the drink. But I still believed him, and the police had nothing to hold him on.

Ricky and Julius were both arrested. Greta was at large. Wesley was released and promised the police he would return to Seattle.

Loren Scranton remained a big question mark.

Mickey, Luis, and I were back at my parents' house, again, another late night. We were all drinking bourbon and feeling spent. We had filled Mom and Dad in on what occurred at the hospital, though we left out a lot of the details, including the part about my stabbing Julius in the cheek with a chopstick. I could hardly think about it myself, let alone tell them.

Mickey and I didn't tell anyone about getting married, either. It was our own sweet secret for the time being.

I was still a little wobbly. I'd been in Portland for a week, and it felt like a month, with all that had happened. Luis decided to go home the next day. Mickey and I thought we'd stick around for a couple of days, to see if we could have some "normal" visiting time with Mom and Dad.

"Normal" went out the window when Mom said, "But what about Claudia? We can't drop this yet. She's in danger, even though she won't tell anyone who's threatening her."

I took a sip of my drink. "Mom, what is this 'we' stuff?"

She shrugged. "Darling, your father and I are involved, whether you like it or not. We still don't know who the hell Loren Scranton is."

"I'm fine with believing that he's a wacko accountant who fell in love with you at first sight."

"Bullmarkey," Mom muttered.

Dad laughed. "I haven't heard that in a while! You used to say that, muffin, when you were young. Mixed up 'bullshit' with 'malarkey.' Of course, I have no idea where you learned cuss words like that when you were little." He winked.

Mom sighed. "Doesn't anyone agree with me? There are still questions we need to answer."

Mickey leaned forward. "I agree with you, Sylvia. The Big-elows are in town until the day after tomorrow. Why don't we meet with them and Claudia once more before they head back to Seattle?"

I groaned. "Fine. But I don't think we should delay Luis from getting home to Ruby."

Luis smiled. "I can take a later flight tomorrow, after we meet with the Bigelows."

Dad stood up. "Good. Then it's settled."

"Except for one detail!" I stood up, too. "You and Mom are not coming with us."

Dad held out his hand to shake mine. "Agreed." We shook.

"Apparently I don't get a say in this agreement?" Mom asked.

"Really, Mom? You really *want* to go?"

She paused. "No. I just want answers."

I called Nancy Bigelow first thing in the morning and asked if we could meet to make sure that they knew what happened at the hospital, in case the police weren't thorough. It was a lame reason to get together, but she pounced on it and seemed eager, in fact, to see us.

"Phillip is here now. He canceled his Miami trip and drove down last night. He'll be grateful for the recap. What time?"

So we set it up for two o'clock, and that meant the five of us could have brunch at Mother's Bistro downtown, which, according to Mom and Dad, had the best brunch in Portland. Miraculously, again, according to them, there wasn't a line and we got right in. My parents clearly were regulars—more than one waiter and busser stopped by our table to say hello. It was fun, and I was happy again to see them so settled in their new community.

I stuffed myself with *migas*—scrambled eggs with onions, peppers, tortillas, salsa—they were almost as good as Mickey's cheesy scrambies.

Okay, they were better, but don't tell him I said that.

We left sated and satisfied and had time to stop into Powell's Bookstore before seeing the Bigelows. The store takes up a full city block and is a maze of millions of books, new and used. You truly can get lost in this store. In fact, they have maps so that you can find your way through the different sections, though I think part of the charm is the getting-lost part. We meandered around for about forty-five minute before Luis said it was time to go. Mom and Dad had ventured off to look at cookbooks, so I went to find them to let them know we were leaving.

Of course, I couldn't find them, since I couldn't find the cookbooks section. My map of the store was in Mickey's back pocket. I eventually asked a Powell's employee, who pointed me to the Orange Room, and that's when I saw Mom and Dad.

And Loren Scranton, his arm in a sling and his suit still fancy.

They hadn't seen me yet. I texted Mickey: "Scranton with 'rents in cookbooks."

It looked like Scranton was pleading with my parents. They didn't seem scared, but they looked uncomfortable, like they didn't want to hear what he was saying. I edged closer to listen, keeping out of sight behind a bookcase.

"We don't have it. It's with the police. Now, you have a choice. Either get out of here quick, or stick around while I call the cops to come pick you up." Dad was using his Martin-Sheen-as-president-in-"The-West-Wing" voice.

I stepped out from behind the bookshelves. "And I should probably warn you, Scranton, that two very pissed-off private investigators are finding their way here as we speak. If I were you, I'd definitely not *ándale, malo man*. I'd stay put, *comprende*?"

He regarded me for an instant, definitely not *comprende*-ing, and then darted away from us, disappearing into the bowels of Powell's.

"'Not *ándale, malo man*'?" Mom asked.

"Don't move, bad guy. Are you two all right?"

Dad was clenching his fists. "He was looking for the gun. Said that he was supposed to pick up the backpack and deliver it."

"Holy moly. To Claudia?" All along we'd assumed that Ricky left the backpack at the airport for Claudia to retrieve herself.

"He didn't say."

Before they could continue, Mickey and Luis came hustling in. "He's gone?" Mickey asked.

I pointed down a hallway. "He ran that way. Turns out he's involved." I hardly got that much out before they were both tearing down the same hall after Scranton.

"This might take a while," I said. "They could be casing this mammoth store for several hours."

"Well, at least we're rid of Scranton now. He knows we don't have the gun. I can't imagine why he would bother us again." Mom sighed deeply. "Another mystery solved. Come on, let's buy these books for the bakery and then you can go see the Bigelows, once Crockett and Tubbs get back."

"Mom! You slay me! 'Miami Vice'?"

"They were my favorite TV duo. I meant that as the highest of compliments."

There was a convenient check-out counter in the Orange Room, and an exit onto the street. I went outside to wait, hoping to catch a glimpse of Mickey and Luis. Turned out they were right there, waiting for us.

"He got away, or he's hiding in this store somewhere," Mickey told me.

"You going to tell Dawson and Monroe?"

"Just texted Dawson."

Chapter Twenty-eight

Mom and Dad went home while Mickey, Luis, and I proceeded to The Nines Hotel to see the Bigelows—all three of them.

When Nancy greeted us in the lobby, she was alone. "We have a suite upstairs. Why don't we go up and wait for Phil and Claudia? They should be back soon. I think they just went for a walk."

We followed her into the elevator and into a spacious suite with living room and dining room areas, and a spectacular view of the city. It occurred to me that ball bearings must be a fruitful industry. Either that or this family had money that actually did grow on trees.

"This is very beautiful," commented Luis.

"The Jacuzzi bathtub is my favorite pleasure!" exclaimed Nancy, clapping her hands together like a seven-year-old who just got a puppy for Christmas. She seemed to be pushing her happiness button a little too hard.

"Please, sit." She motioned to the sectional couch. "Can I get you all something to drink?"

"No thanks," responded Mickey. "How's Claudia doing?"

Nancy sat up straight, pressing her hands against her knees, big smile on her face. "She's great. Really really great. I'm so proud of her, the way she has pulled through this horrible mess."

"Did she tell you any more about the gun, and why she wanted it?" I asked.

The big smile got littler. "No, but whatever that was all about, it seems like it's behind her now."

"Forgive me, Mrs. Bigelow, but I would suggest that you be worried about your daughter. It is a serious thing when a young person is planning to shoot someone." Luis tilted his head. "You might want to get her some counseling, yes?"

Nancy emitted a nervous giggle a la Jennifer Lawrence. "Oh, I don't think she'll need counseling, really. She has us, and her friends, and she'll come out of this just fine, I'm sure of it, really."

When someone says "really" over and over again, I start thinking that what they're saying is anything but real.

"Mind if I use a bathroom?" I stood up, and Nancy pointed to a side door. "The half bath is right in there, dear."

"Oh," I tried a little giggle myself. "Would it be all right if I use the full bathroom, so that I can see the Jacuzzi?"

"Of course! Right down the hall, off the bedroom."

I didn't care one bubble about the Jacuzzi, but Nancy was acting so jittery that I thought I would make sure Claudia wasn't lying in bed. If Nancy had stopped me from going to the full bathroom, I would have known something was up. Anyway, there I was, scouting the super fancy hotel digs, making my way to the toilet. I flushed it and then ran some water in the sink, like I was washing my hands. I peeked into a vanity bag—makeup, toothpaste, a couple of pill bottles, etc.—and turned off the faucet. On my way back out, I saw Phillip's briefcase open and noticed a bunch of papers and file folders.

I was about to return to the living room when I halted and backed up.

There was a piece of paper I recognized.

A crumpled note.

It was the one that had been left in Claudia's hospital room.

I picked it up, shoved it in my pocket, and collected my wits before rejoining the others.

It turns out that I'm not so good at collecting my wits.

"Nancy! What is going on?" I demanded.

Mickey and Luis jolted. Nancy put her palm to her chest. "Why, whatever do you mean, dear?"

I pulled the note out and shook it out in front of her. "This note!"

She froze momentarily and then grabbed it out of my hands.

"Babe, what is that?"

"Mickey, I just found this in Phillip's briefcase! It's the one that was in…"

"It was in Claudia's hospital bedside table," interrupted Nancy. "I know. I'm the one who took it."

"You didn't say a word about it when I asked Claudia about it at the hospital. You were standing right there!"

"I was hoping she would explain who gave it to her, but as you remember, she wasn't explaining anything at all!" Nancy's cheerful mask had given way to a pained and angry expression. She was practically baring her teeth at me.

"Why was it in Phillip's briefcase?" Mickey asked, calmly, trying to talk me down with his eyes.

"Oh, for heaven's sake, I don't know. I tossed it in there, I guess." She walked to the picture window and gazed out over Portland.

"Except," I said quietly, locking my eyes on Mickey's, "Phillip just got here from Miami. Are you saying you held on to this note for the past however many days, took it to Seattle with you, and then just plopped it in his briefcase, um, today? Yesterday? When, exactly?"

Nancy was quiet. Luis joined her at the window. "Mrs. Bigelow, we want to help. Do you know who wrote the note? Are you trying to protect someone?"

She burst into tears and flung herself on Luis, sobbing into his shoulder. He patted her gently on the back and muttered "*díos mío*" just loud enough for us to hear.

She wailed better than Sally Fields in *Steel Magnolias,* only I wasn't feeling much of the love. I brought her a tissue, and she soon disengaged from Luis and blew her nose. I wasn't buying her distress performance any more than I bought her sunshine act.

We all sat down again. Nancy sat close to Luis on the couch; Mickey and I faced them. "Are you ready to tell us?" asked Mickey.

"Oh, yes, yes, I think so, I really do," she gushed.

There was that word again. Really.

Chapter Twenty-nine

Nancy relayed a story to us that is a common, horrible nightmare, one that happens way too much in too many families all over the globe. About three months ago, she had started suspecting that her husband had been abusing Claudia. She noticed that Claudia was avoiding him, and given his propensity for young women (her words, not mine), she began to worry about her daughter's safety. But, she said, Claudia would not talk to her about any of it and insisted that her father wasn't doing anything wrong.

"And then *this* disaster"—she flung her arms out on the word "this" and practically took Luis' nose off with her megadiamond ring—"and if it's true that Wesley is not to blame, well, then I simply have to think it's my Phillip!" This brought her to tears again. She rushed out of the room to the bathroom.

Now, I am disgusted by any father who would treat his daughter with anything but love and respect. I have the greatest father in the world. I can't imagine being afraid of him causing me any kind of bodily harm. And I already thought that Phillip Bigelow was a sleazemonger. But Nancy seemed so fake. My gut was churning with doubt.

I shook my head at Luis and Mickey. "I don't know," I whispered. "This doesn't feel right to me, this story."

"We have to follow up, no matter what," Mickey whispered back.

Luis and I both nodded. "Do we wait here, or go see if we can find them?"

Nancy returned, pressing a damp washcloth to her forehead. "I need a drink. Can I get you all something?" Her voice was surprisingly steady.

"No, thank you, Nancy. Look, do you know where Claudia and Phil went? Are you worried that she's in danger right now?" asked Mickey.

Nancy turned her back to fix a drink at the small bar. "Oh, I doubt he would try anything out in the big, wide, world, if you know what I mean. Phil does things behind closed doors." She poured what sounded like a generous amount of scotch into a glass and faced us. She took a swallow. "Anyway, I don't know where they are." She took another swallow. "It's a relief to get this off my chest, I can tell you that." Another swallow.

"What's your plan, Nancy? Are you going to confront Phillip?" I asked.

She sat back down next to Luis. "He'll just deny it, and Claudia won't turn on him, so I think I should get Claudia out of the house, away from him. I think she likes it here. Maybe I can set her up down here. Have her transfer to Portland State. That would get her away from both Phil and that Wesley moron." Another swallow.

For all of the things one might be able to call Wesley, he didn't strike me as a moron. I wondered what the hell Claudia's parents had against him. Maybe Wesley really did hit Claudia once? I didn't think so. Maybe Nancy was wishing she was Mrs. Robinson, able to seduce the young Wesley a la Dustin Hoffman in *The Graduate,* only Wesley wouldn't have her. And why did people stay married who were so unhappy with each other? And why would a mother stay with a husband who was abusing their child?

Mickey interrupted my reverie. "Nancy, it turns out that Loren Scranton was supposed to retrieve the backpack with the gun. Are you sure you've never heard of him? Is it possible that Claudia knows him?"

Nancy brushed a wayward lock of hair away from her face and leaned back against the couch. "I don't know everyone she knows. I have never heard of this guy, I can promise you that." She jabbed her finger in the air at Mickey.

She was drunk. I now understood that she had started in on the scotch well before we arrived.

Luis stood up. "I suggest we wait for Mr. Bigelow and Claudia in the lobby, and let Mrs. Bigelow get some rest."

Mickey and I couldn't stand up too quickly. "Good idea," we responded in unison.

"Really? You can stay here if you'd like. Have a drink. We'll toast our miseries together." She held up her glass to us.

We all made our way to the door. "We'll be in the lobby, and we'll keep you posted. Call Annabelle on her cell if you hear from them. You take care of yourself." Mickey gave her a little smile, and we were outta there.

"Yuck," I sputtered, as we got on the elevator. "I feel like I need a bath."

"Jacuzzi?" Mickey joked.

"Anything but. Did you buy any of that? Or all of it? Or…?"

"Hard to discount it, but mostly, I think it was bullmarkey." Luis grinned.

I elbowed Mickey. "I'm never going to hear the end of that, I bet."

Mickey took my hand as the elevator doors opened. "It's my new favorite word."

We wanted to have a drink in the lobby—in fact, even Luis said, "We need a drink"—but we immediately realized that Phillip and Claudia could take the elevator from the street level straight up to the room, the lobby being on the eighth floor. I also espied the billiards room, part of the super cool lobby, and had a yen to see if I still had my recent magic touch, but all of this was out of the question if we were to apprehend Phillip. So we got on the elevator again and disembarked at street level.

It was chilly and windy. The doormen greeted us like lost friends (it became clearer and clearer to me each day in Portland that they must have a law about providing the friendliest customer service in the world), but it was awkward to loiter on the street.

"I wish I had my sock-monkey hat."

"Oh, gosh, yes, we so wish you had it too," Mickey quipped.

"*Amiga*, call Claudia on her phone, why don't you?"

"I was just about to do that, *mi bueno cómplice*."

Luis cracked up. "I am your accomplice? I believe that means we are partners in crime, no?"

Mickey laughed. "Not far off."

I found Claudia's number on my incoming call log and punched it. The three of us were mulling around in small circles, trying to stay warm. The phone rang four times before she answered. "Hello?"

"Claudia, it's Annabelle. Are you all right?"

"Yes."

"Are you with your father?"

"Yes."

"Is he all right?"

"What do you mean?"

"I mean, is he treating you all right?"

"OH GOD. WHAT DID SHE TELL YOU?" Claudia screamed into the phone. "I CAN'T BELIEVE THIS!"

"It's okay, calm down. We want to help you. Where's your father right now?"

"He's in the men's room. We just got out from the movies. God!"

"Where are you?"

"I'm not telling, Annabelle. You are not going to do anything, okay? I don't need your help anymore!"

"Claudia, did you want the gun to kill your father?"

A pause. "You have no idea." She hung up.

I threw my hands up in the air. "Jeez Louise, what are supposed to do now?" I told them what she said.

Mickey ran his hands through his hair. "I'm starting to be very sick of the sicko Bigelows. If she doesn't want our help, maybe we should go back upstairs and have that drink."

"But Mickey, if she's really in trouble…"

"I know, I know."

Luis looked around, held out his finger signaling us to wait a second, and approached a doorman. He came back to us and pointed up the street. "The closest movie theater is that way a couple of blocks. I say we go there."

We set off in a jog toward the marquee lit up with *Dumb and Dumber To, A Most Violent Year, Sex Tape,* and *Gone Girl.* I didn't want to think about father and daughter Bigelow seeing any of those together.

Chapter Thirty

There's a lyric in a Mumford and Sons song that asks what the fault is in giving one's whole heart. There's another lyric on the same album where the singer confesses that he really fucked things up.

Well, both applied to me as we approached the crowd spilling out of the movie theater complex. I was determined, with all my heart, to save Claudia from her disgusting father, in spite of her denials. Then I really fucked things up.

Mickey, Luis, and I all saw Claudia and Phillip at the same time, and we dodged and darted between the movie-goers, trying to get to them. It looked to me like Claudia was crying, and that Phillip had a firm grip on her arm.

So I shouted her name as loud as I could, along with "STOP!"

The crowd, as though choreographed, came to a dead stop, looking around for whoever Claudia was. She didn't stop, however. She and Phillip sped up, in fact, heading across the street for what looked like an elevator shaft. Mickey, Luis, and I ran toward them, but they reached the elevator doors before us and got on just before they closed. They were headed to an underground parking garage.

Mickey tossed me a look of frustration. "Annabelle, why did you yell? We could have gotten to them!"

Luis kept punching the down arrow, but said nothing.

"Well, gee, Mickey, I didn't know they were going underground!"

"Babe, it's like bad movies, when the cops need to bust into an apartment to arrest a drug dealer and they show up with ten squad cars and sirens blazing. And then the drug dealer gets away. Right?"

"You want me to be stealthier."

"Please."

"Roger that."

Mickey sighed. "It's okay. We'll find them."

When the elevator door opened, we all stood there, realizing we had no idea what floor Phillip and Claudia had descended to.

Luis led the charge back across the street and around a corner to the exit for the garage. We stood watching cars coming out, and I, for one, didn't know what we were to do should we see father and daughter. Jump on the car's hood? Throw ourselves in front of the car? Shoot the tires? "Mickey, what are we supposed to do?"

"We'll see if we can stop them," was his vague reply. Then he motioned to Luis, pointing into the garage. "Annabelle, you stay here, we'll go inside."

I was thinking, okay, this is right, I should hang back and let the two ex-cop PIs handle the situation, but I was feeling a bit patronized. I mean, Mickey was right, I shouldn't have shouted, but it was a little mistake, and I've gotten myself and Mickey out of lots of tricky situations.

So when I saw a black Range Rover with Washington plates emerging, with Phillip and Claudia sitting in front, I stopped thinking. As the car slowed down before entering the street, I threw the first thing I grabbed out of my purse.

It was my Katharine Hepburn biography.

It thudded and bounced off the windshield.

"What the hell do you think you're doing?" The man driving roared out the window.

The man who wasn't Phillip.

I rushed to pick up my book, apologizing like crazy. "So sorry. I thought you were someone else. Your windshield looks fine. No damage done. So so sorry." I smiled meekly.

He huffed and drove off.

I repositioned myself by the door and saw a Portland police officer walking toward me.

Oh, great.

"You having a problem, miss?"

I shook my head energetically. "No, sir, no, I simply was attempting to get the attention of someone, but it turned out to be the wrong someone. No harm done, just an unfortunate incident, that's all." I smiled broadly.

He didn't. "You're lucky he didn't stick around to press charges."

"I am indeed, very lucky, yes sir." Still smiling.

He wasn't impressed. "I'd like to see your identification."

I stopped smiling and pulled out my wallet and license. He studied it and handed it back to me. "How long are you in town?"

"I promise I'll leave as soon as possible, probably another couple of days."

"No more book-throwing, okay?"

"Ten four."

The officer returned to his patrol car down the street, and I peered around the corner into the garage, hoping to espy Mickey or Luis. Where the hell were they? At least they hadn't witnessed that latest screw-up of mine. I seemed to be on a roll.

That's when a dark blue Mercedes came screeching out with Mickey and Luis running behind it.

I still had the book in my hand, so I threw it again. This time it flew in through the open window on the driver's side and hit him in the head.

Phillip.

It surprised him enough that he slammed on the brakes and stopped long enough for Mickey to run up to the door, reach in and grab his shoulder and yell, "Cut the engine, now!"

Luis was on the other side but couldn't open the locked door.

Phillip put the Mercedes in park and turned off the engine.

Drivers behind him started honking.

Mickey yelled again. "Get out. I'll pull the car over."

Mickey can be very convincing. Phillip got out.

Luis came around and took Phillip by the arm, while Mickey parked the car on a block away. Luis, Phillip, and I walked up to meet him.

I neglected to tell you…Claudia was not in the car.

Phillip was silent. I wasn't. "Where is she, Phillip? Where's Claudia? She was with you just a few minutes ago! Did you hurt her?"

This last question made him wince, but he didn't answer me.

Mickey stuck the Mercedes keys in his pocket and came up close to Phillip's face. "You want to talk to us first, or do you want us to take you right to the police?"

"There happens to be a cop nearby. I happened to, um, meet him earlier."

Mickey frowned at me. "What?"

"Never mind. Phillip, listen to Mickey. You should talk to us first."

Phillip tried to wrest his arm away from Luis. "Not yet, *señor*. We need answers first. We believe you know why your daughter needed that gun."

Bigelow sneered. "I don't give a rat's ass what you believe. You've got no right invading my family's privacy. Let me go, and I won't press charges for assault."

"In your dreams, dirtwad," I assured him.

"Us, or the police, Phil? I'm waiting for your answer." Luis was firm.

"You," he finally answered.

"At the hotel suite?"

"Sure. Why the fuck not? Let's go."

We walked the few blocks to The Nines. I called Claudia on the way, but she wasn't answering.

My Hepburn biography was back in my purse, dented and dirtied, but intact and as sturdy as she was. I think she would have liked to know that her book had more than one story to its name. Then I recalled Drew's story about Sal being attacked with a book by a homophobe. Maybe that was my unconscious inspiration. I'd have to tell him.

We got back to the hotel and rode the elevator up to the suite. Phillip had a key and let us in.

The lights were all off.

On turning one on and surveying the bedroom and bathrooms it was clear to all of us.

Nancy was gone.

Chapter Thirty-one

"I have never hurt my daughter," repeated Phillip for the umpteenth time.

"That's not what Nancy told us," Mickey said, also for the umpteenth time. "Aren't you tired of going around and around on this, Phil? Aren't you worried about Claudia? Do you even know where she is?"

He shook his head. "She ran away from me when we came out of the elevator to the parking garage."

"What movie did you see, by the way?" I asked.

"*Gone Girl.*"

"That must have really cheered her up," I sneered.

He shrugged. "She picked it."

"Appropriate, I guess, given the current circumstances," suggested Mickey.

I kept dialing Claudia, every five minutes or so. Still no answer.

"Mr. Bigelow, you told us that you wanted to talk to us, but you are not talking to us. I am thinking we should call the police, Mick, *sí?* This is getting us nowhere."

Phillip sat up straight. "You have nothing to tell the police. All you have is the word of my wife, and as you can see, she is nowhere in sight. My guess is she is on her way back to Seattle."

"With Claudia?"

Another shrug. "I hope not."

"Why is that, Phillip?" I asked.

He gave me one of his sleazy leers. "You already think I'm a rapist. You probably think every man who looks at you twice is a rapist. I know your type, girlie."

I jumped up and started toward him but Luis stepped in and held me back. They both know that I can handle being called just about anything but "girlie."

"Mickey, let's call Dawson and Monroe. Let's get rid of this dirtbag. Wherever Claudia is, she's better off than with him."

I turned on my heel and stalked off to the Jacuzzi bathroom to collect myself. I took the opportunity to call Mom and Dad to let them know we were okay and that we'd probably be home in an hour or so, after we deposited Phillip at the police station.

I hung up, washed my face with some fancy smelly soap and dried it on a plush white towel. I opened the drawers in the vanity and saw nothing but the hotel's hair dryer. I didn't know what I was looking for, other than some kind of clue, any kind of clue, as to Phillip's guilt or Nancy's whereabouts. We had already looked through Nancy's suitcase, which looked nicely packed and ready to go, until we messed with it. But nothing turned up there, either.

Then I noticed the shelf under the sink and squatted down to take a look. There were two bottles of pills, maybe the ones I had seen on my last visit to this suite. This time I read the labels. They were prescriptions for Claudia. One was clozapine. The other was for lithium.

I didn't know what clozapine was. Lithium, I thought, was for treating bipolar disorder.

Great. Claudia was a certified nutcase, thanks to her perv Dad.

I was walking out into the hallway leading to the living area when my phone vibrated. It was a text from Claudia.

I'm with Mom. Meet us outside the hotel. Come alone. We have Mom's car.

I couldn't go and not tell Luis and Mickey. I didn't want Phillip to hear, though, so I motioned Mickey to come into the bathroom. I told him about the pills and showed him the text. "What do you think? I should go, right?"

Mickey scowled. "I don't know. I don't like the idea of you going alone."

"We need to make sure Claudia is okay. I'll be fine. Maybe I can talk her into going to the police. I'll let them know that we have Phillip."

Mickey nodded. "All right. Keep me posted. We'll wait here at least until we hear from you." He kissed me. "Be careful. Do you have your weapon?"

"Huh?"

"That book. You have a good arm. Who knew?" He kissed me again.

"You should see my glider."

He smiled. "I think you mean slider."

"Whatever." I hugged him, nodded to Luis on my way out, and took the elevator down to the street.

Sure enough, Claudia and Nancy were waiting for me in a Honda CRV. Nancy was in the driver's seat. Claudia climbed out, opened the back door, and directed me to climb in.

With a gun in her hand.

In some situations, I'm actually very good at doing what I'm told.

Chapter Thirty-two

Mickey and I had established a routine a few months earlier. We don't say "hello" when we answer each other's call, if we're in trouble. We keep the line open, and the one calling knows to listen, to hear any clues about what might be going on.

As soon as Claudia slammed the back door—after first explaining if I tried to run, she'd shoot me, right then and there—my phone rang. I pulled it out of my pocket and saw that it was Mickey.

"Don't answer that!" Claudia waved her gun at me.

I swiped it like I was hanging up, but I was answering it. Just not with "hello." I put it back in my purse but close to the top, hoping the light of the phone wouldn't be seen.

Throwing my book again didn't seem like a good idea, so I started to babble, which is what I do when I don't know what else to do. "Claudia, where are we going? We have your father at the hotel. He can't hurt you anymore, and if he even tried, I bet Luis or Mickey would make sure he walked funny for the rest of his life, if you know what I mean. All I've done is try to help you, and your mother knows the secret about nasty ole Phillip, so I think you can walk away from all of this, maybe see a therapist, put your dad in jail, even lock him up yourself, like in that movie *The Secret in Their Eyes*? Did you see it? It was from Argentina, I think, and it had this great ending, which I sort of already blew just telling you this but…"

"Shut up, Annabelle whatsyourname with the dentist's business card." She held the gun on me, but I could see that her hand was shaking.

I was feeling shaky myself, so I sat on my hands. "What about you, Nancy? Do you know where we're going?"

Nancy had pulled out into the street and was turning to head toward the Willamette River. "If I were you, Annabelle, I'd keep my mouth shut." She sounded surprisingly calm. "And, yes, I did see that movie. Subtitles."

Nancy was clearly an astute critic of the cinema.

We continued onto a bridge and I leaned forward to read the signs. "Okay, it looks like we're getting onto Highway 5 north. Are we going to Seattle? And is this your Honda CRV, Nancy, or is it a rental? Nice silver color. Any reason you both need me to go with you, at gunpoint? Because, really, I'm good to go, if you want to let me out anywhere..."

"I want you to stop talking *now*, do you understand?" Claudia's hand was still shaking. She repositioned herself so that she could hold the gun with two hands and point it at my head.

"Yes." I shut up. I figured I had given Mickey as much information as possible. I just hoped he had been able to hear me over the phone.

We merged onto the highway, but quickly exited onto Route 84 east. "Did you know that Route 84, even though it's an interstate highway, doesn't actually go all the way across the country?"

Claudia ignored me and turned on the radio, loud. John Fogerty was singing "Bad Moon Rising."

I'm not kidding.

Then she reached over and took her purse from beside me on the backseat, took out her phone, and dropped the purse on the floor in front of her. She checked for messages or whatever with one hand, while keeping the gun pointed at me, sort of, with the other.

We exited 84 somewhere, but it felt like we were still heading east. I saw a sign that read "Blue Lake, 3 miles."

Claudia was looking straight ahead now. I dug into my purse and swiped the phone off, hit my text icon, chose Mickey at the top of the list, typed in "blue lake," and hit "send." I stuck the phone in my pocket.

The radio was blasting. This time it was Pharrell Williams singing "Happy." I happen to love that song, and I don't care how tired you might be of it, it's a pretty damn near irresistible ditty, in my opinion, and it was giving me some measure of strength in that moment.

Nancy drove into a driveway, parked in a lot, and killed the engine. Claudia turned around toward me. "Get out."

I didn't like this one bit. I didn't understand one bit of it, either. How had I become the enemy? All I did was end up with a gun that wasn't mine, and now I was kidnapped a second time in a week, this time by a skinny white girl.

A young, scared, emotionally sick white girl.

From a rich family in Seattle.

With messed-up parents.

She's not going to kill me, I thought. *She can't be a good shot, and she can't see too well in the dark. And I bet her hands are still shaking.*

I grabbed my purse strap.

"Hurry up, Annabelle." Claudia opened the door for me.

Such a thoughtful young woman.

Nancy was already closing the driver-side door when I leaped out and flung my purse at Claudia.

And I ran.

Some of the park's paths were lit with streetlamps. I avoided them, seeking the darkest areas for cover. I didn't hear anyone following me, but I was running my ass off and couldn't hear much except for my own fierce panting and boots hitting the pavement.

I made it to a densely wooded area and huddled behind a row of bushes.

My ears were as alert as a doberman's (at least mine weren't pointy), but I heard nothing except some rustling of branches. I briefly worried about bears or wolverines or mountain lions or rabid badgers or crazy hyenas in this neck of the country but concentrated instead on David Straithairn, who kept out of sight in *The River Wild* while tracking his wife and son who were held hostage.

That wasn't helping to decrease my panic, so I pulled out my phone to see if I could reach Mickey.

Then I definitely heard something.

A gunshot.

Then silence.

I dialed Mickey.

No service.

I huddled with my coat wrapped around me like a cocoon, wishing I was wrapped in Mickey's arms in our bed in New York City instead. I've never missed my sock-monkey hat so much in my life. My poufy coat was nice and warm, but it didn't do anything for my oversized lotus-leaf ears, which felt like they were hardening faster than super glue in the chilly wind.

I didn't know whether to stay put—would anyone ever find me, before I turned into a poufy-coated, hatless statue?—or to head back to the parking lot.

I decided that movement was called for.

I've already said that I'm a fast runner, but I'm not particularly stealthy. In fact, I would say that "stealth" is not anywhere on my character description, should I be featured in a dictionary. But I tried to be quiet as I darted from behind tree to behind tree to behind park building. At one point I got down on my stomach and crawled military-style—or at least, what I thought was military-style, not ever having been in the military—trying not to groan and whimper as I did.

I finally got close enough to the parking lot to see that the Honda CRV was gone. That had to mean that both Nancy and Claudia had left, or one of them was gone and the other one was shot.

I figured Nancy was shot, since Claudia had the gun.

Was she lying dead somewhere, or sitting up somewhere, or wandering aimlessly, half dead, like a character in *Pineapple*

Express where everyone gets shot at the end but the good guys…? Never mind. I won't tell you the ending.

This made me realize that I no longer knew who the good guys were. Except for me and Mickey and Luis and Mom and Dad, of course.

I crouched beside a trash can, rubbing my hands, and peering around its side. The lights that illuminated the walkways helped me see a little bit in all directions.

Then I heard a moan.

I inched my way forward and risked calling out. "Where are you?"

Another moan.

I made my way toward it, carefully, aware that the moaner could be armed. Maybe everyone in the Bigelow family was a card-carrying member of the NRA.

I saw a figure, sitting and leaning against a wooden building.

It wasn't Nancy, and it wasn't Claudia.

But it *was* a member of the NRA.

It was Loren Scranton.

Chapter Thirty-three

Scranton was not hurt badly. Even I, unseasoned detective that I was, could see that. His upper arm—not the one that was already broken—was bleeding, but not a lot. I lifted it away from him and could see that there was no real bullet hole and no exit hole, either.

"Just a scratch," I told him, trying to come off as cool as Susan Sarandon in *Thelma and Louise* and using a line from, oh, probably a hundred movies. "What are you doing here? Who are you, and I mean, for real?"

"Followed you here."

"You've been following us everywhere. I'm more than a little sick of you."

"The backpack. The police really have it?"

"Why should I talk to you about any of this, until you tell me what's going on?"

"So how did she end up with the gun?"

"Like I said, you hear nothing from me until you give me something." My voice was quivering, but I hoped I was keeping it under control. I knew Mickey would show up soon, as long as my phone had been in service for the duration of the ride to the park.

I saw my purse on the ground, where I had hurled it at Claudia. I retrieved it and looked inside. Nothing missing.

I crouched in front of Scranton. "You were supposed to retrieve the backpack? That's why you were talking to me and Mom at baggage claim?"

He nodded.

"Ricky set that up?"

"I don't know any Ricky."

"So who told you to get the gun and give it to Claudia?"

He moaned again.

"Buck up, Scranton. Like I said, I'm sick of you, and I've already hit two people tonight using a book and a purse." I shivered.

"I wasn't supposed to give it to Claudia."

"Hmm. Okay. So who were you supposed to give it to?"

He closed his eyes. "Phillip Bigelow."

That's when I heard a car approaching, fast, and that's when I sat down and leaned against the same building, next to Loren Scranton.

I was exhausted.

◇◇◇

Mickey ripped Scranton's sleeve off from his shirt and wrapped it tightly around his arm. I guess it was bleeding more than I thought. They were in the backseat of Dad's car. Luis was driving, and I was navigating, using a map on my iPhone. We were taking Scranton to the hospital, where Dawson and Monroe would meet us.

Scranton told us that Phillip asked him to get the gun so that his daughter wouldn't get it.

"How did he know Claudia was getting a gun?" Mickey asked.

"Somehow he hacks her phone account. Reads her texts."

"Why you?" Mickey continued.

"Phil found out about the drop before it was going to happen. He was in Miami. He knew I was due in Portland. He booked a flight for me so that I'd land at the airport at the right time. Actually, Phil made *sure* it would be the right time. Texted Ricky, as Claudia, to have the backpack ready for pick up when my flight landed, which was earlier than what Claudia had previously arranged. So by the time she got to the airport, I would have gotten the gun."

My opinion of Phillip Bigelow had not improved. What sort of creeptard father hacks his kid's phone?

"Why did Claudia shoot you?"

Scranton shook his head. "She didn't. Nancy did."

I twirled around in my seat. "Nancy had the gun?"

He nodded.

"Claudia had it when I ran."

"I came up on them after that. Nancy had it." He paused. "She told me to leave them alone. I told her to put the gun down. She shot me."

Mickey sat back in the seat. "Aren't you an accountant? What is all this? Why didn't you just let this go, once you didn't have the backpack? You've been stalking us ever since."

"And how did you know I had the gun?" I added.

"The cricket."

"What cricket?" Mickey asked, exasperated.

"The silver charm on Annabelle's backpack. I noticed it on the plane. After you and your folks left the airport, I realized the backpack I was to retrieve wasn't there. I waited around, thinking Ricky was late in the delivery. Then I saw Claudia come in and grab a backpack that was close to the drop-off point. When she took it, I saw the cricket. I put two and two together." He rubbed his arm. "Phil called me on Tuesday morning, told me Claudia had been mugged. He didn't know then that the police had the gun. I told him I'd find you, to see if you had it. He didn't want it connected to his daughter in any way. I remembered what your mother said about where you lived. I was driving on your street on Tuesday when I saw you driving the other way. I followed you but lost you in the Pearl. Eventually I found you, and then, well, I got hit by that car." He took a deep breath. "After that, I couldn't get in touch with Phil, so I kept trying to meet up with you."

"He left his phone in Miami when he came to Portland, that's why," I explained. "How and why did you follow us to Blue Lake?" I added.

"I finally located Phil. Called around to the hotels."

"Doesn't he have an office? An assistant? You could have contacted him that way?"

"Not supposed to. He's strict about that and wants me to contact him only on his cell."

We all digested this for a moment before Scranton continued.

"I was worried about the whole situation. I went to see Claudia in the hospital on Friday. I stayed only a couple of minutes after a nurse asked me who I was. I still couldn't reach Phil. So by Sunday evening I decided to try to see him. Thought I'd call him from the lobby. I came up right when you were pulling out."

"Again," Mickey said, "why stay involved?"

"I owe Phillip."

"How? Why?"

"We've done, uh, business together a long time."

This was reason for another digestive pause. I decided I didn't want to know any more about Phillip Bigelow's accounting practices.

Luis was getting off Highway 84 at the Forty-third Street exit. We were heading to Providence Hospital. "The *señora* told us she had never heard of you."

"She is probably telling the truth. She and Claudia have never met me. I bet Phil doesn't talk to them about finances..." He trailed off.

Mickey reached up to squeeze my shoulder. "You okay?"

"Just wondering where the gun came from, the one Claudia has now. Or Nancy. Or whoever."

Luis pulled into the emergency room lot, where Dawson and Monroe were waiting for us. We all walked Scranton inside, and a nurse led him to a seat. Dawson regarded Mickey. "You want to do this now or later?"

"Nice of you to ask. I appreciate that. If we could reconvene in the morning, that would be best. I think Annabelle here could use a hot bath and some food." He put his arm around me. "But you've got the info on the Honda, right? With Claudia and Nancy Bigelow? They've got a gun, and we're not sure why."

Dawson nodded. "We've got an APB out. We'll question Scranton tonight. You folks are staying in town, yes?"

The three of us answered "yes" in unison.

"Good. At the station, nine o'clock?"

"Thanks." Mickey held out his hand, and Dawson shook it. Monroe was on his phone and gave a little wave as we left.

On the way out of the hospital, I stopped. "Luis! Oh, no! You were going to fly home tonight!"

Luis smiled. "It is okay, *amiga*. I would not leave before knowing that you and your family are okay. I think this is some kind of record, no?"

"What?"

"You've been kidnapped twice in a week!"

That's when my knees buckled and Mickey caught me before I hit the ground. He helped me to the car, and we went home to Mom and Dad's.

Dusty greeted us buoyantly, Mom hugged me hard and told me I looked like shit, Dad poured me a drink, and Mickey stayed right by my side, like we were Siamese twins.

Luis called Ruby. I heard him say, "*Te encantará* Annabelle."

I whispered to Mickey. "She will encounter me?"

He kissed my cheek. "I don't know."

I looked it up later. It meant, "You'll love Annabelle."

Luis. What a guy. All I ever did was get him into trouble, and he figured his wife would love me.

I could only imagine that either Ruby was a pistol, or that Luis didn't know his wife very well.

Chapter Thirty-four

I woke up Monday morning and the first thing I thought of was Bonkers. I had been gone a whole week, and I missed my kitty perching on top of my chest and nose-butting me. Mickey was still asleep, snoring softly, which was not a satisfactory substitute for Bonkers' purrs.

I sat up and found my phone on the bedside table. I texted Vicki, although I knew that Mickey had already told her we didn't know when we'd be back.

"Hi, Vicki. How's the Bonks?" I typed.

I waited, staring at the screen until it dinged.

A picture of Bonkers, sound asleep on Vicki's bed, popped up with a message. "No worries! Eating well, playing with mouse toys, sleeping a lot."

This made me feel better, then made me a little upset. Bonks didn't seem to be missing me at all.

I poked Mickey. "Hey."

He jolted awake, alarmed. "What? Huh? You okay?"

"Jeez, Mickey, I'm just waking you up. It's late." I had no idea what time it was, but it felt late.

Mickey picked up his watch from the other bedside table. "Annabelle, it's six o'clock. Jeez yourself." He lay back down and pulled the covers to his chin. "Go to sleep."

"Can't do that. Bonkers isn't here and Bonkers doesn't miss me."

He coughed. "Bonkers is fine. Vicki said so yesterday."

"I know. She just sent me a picture." I held my phone in front of his face. "Look."

He opened his eyes. "Looks like Bonkers."

"Exactly. I have to go home before he forgets who I am."

Mickey rolled away from me. "I don't think we can go home until Dawson and Monroe are satisfied that we aren't central to their investigation. And besides, don't you want to make sure that Claudia is okay?" He yawned.

"Claudia Schmaudia. She held a gun on me. I think she's wacko. This vacation has not been a vacation at all."

"Good reason to stay a couple of days longer, right? To have some relaxed time with the 'rents before we leave?"

I snuggled up behind him, spooning, and reached my arm across him so that the picture of Bonkers was in front of his face again. "You can resist this perfect kitty?"

He groaned and took my phone. "Absolutely." He put the phone down and then rolled over toward me. "Are you trying to tell me that you need your cat more than you need me?"

We kissed, and then kissed some more, a lot more, and then Mickey pulled me on top of him, and, well, after a little while, I decided it was cool for my cat to have Vicki as a best friend. Sex with Mickey was better without Bonkers watching us from the end of the bed.

A little later we had coffee and toast with Mom, Dad, and Luis, and then set off to the police station for our meeting with Dawson and Monroe.

Dawson greeted us with handshakes. "Nancy Bigelow is here. She called her husband early this morning, asked him to pick her up at the airport. Apparently Claudia dropped her there and drove off."

"Phillip?" Mickey asked.

"He's here, too."

"What about Scranton?"

"All three of them."

"Are they talking? Do they know where Claudia went?"

Dawson shook his head. "No. They say that Claudia is troubled, bipolar or something."

"Where's the gun?" I asked.

"Apparently Claudia has it. Forced her mother out of the car with it. Pointed it at her and told her to walk away or she'd shoot."

I frowned. "But Nancy shot Scranton?"

"Now he's saying he's not sure who shot him."

"You have still the APB out on the car?" Luis asked.

Dawson nodded. "Yes, but no hits. Why don't we all sit down over here and wrap this thing up?" He motioned to a room to our right, and we followed him in. It was an interrogation room. We sat in the chairs around the table in the middle.

"I have some good news. We had another attack in the park. Well, that's not good news, but we caught the guy. He confessed to the assault on Claudia. He was looking to rob her, but there was nothing worth his time in your backpack."

My silver cricket? How could a robber resist that? I thought.

He smiled at me. "Plus, I think you and your folks showed up and he got scared and ran."

"So that had nothing to do with any of this?" I surmised.

"Bingo. And," he reached under the table, "here's your backpack." He handed it to me.

"Thanks." I put it on my lap and rubbed the silver cricket, like that would make me feel better.

"I don't see why you all have to stick around anymore," Dawson continued." Your story about the backpack at the airport and everything that has happened since, it all coincides with what the Bigelows have told us."

"What about this second gun, the one Claudia has now? Do we know where it came from?" I asked.

"No. Phillip never saw Claudia with it, and Nancy says she wouldn't know how to describe a gun accurately, except that it was a pistol. We know that Phillip owns a gun, but he hasn't been home to see if it's still there or not. We'll be checking that out right away."

I sighed. "I wish we knew what was up with Claudia. Why did she take me with them last night? She knows I've just been trying to help. It's so confusing. I hate to leave when everything still feels so unsettled."

"We'll find Claudia, Annabelle. It won't surprise me if we find her today, in fact."

"Would it be possible for us to talk to the Bigelows?"

Mickey extended his hand across the table to me. "Babe, that's not a good idea. We've done what we can for Claudia, and the detective is right. The police will locate the car and then all will be clear."

"I don't want to walk away from this yet."

"What happened to 'Claudia Schmaudia'? I thought you were ready to wash your hands of her and her problems."

"I'm pissed off, Mickey. I need answers. She reached out to me, twice, and then she abducted me. It makes no sense. Maybe she's brainwashed or something…" I trailed off.

"*Amiga,* what can you do at this point anyway?" Luis asked me, calmly.

I didn't have an answer.

Dawson stood. "Thanks, folks. Have a safe trip home to New York. If we need you for anything, we know how to reach you." Another round of handshakes, and we were gone.

On our way out, however, I saw Nancy Bigelow down a hallway, and broke away from Mickey's side to approach her. "Nancy!" I called.

She stopped and turned. "Oh, it's you!" She fidgeted with her purse. "I was just going to the ladies room." I noticed a uniformed officer further down the hall, watching her, and now us.

"Just wondering if you have anything you'd like to tell me, seeing as how we were all in a park last night with a gun, and, oh yeah, you and your daughter kidnapped me, remember?"

I could hear Mickey approaching me, as I saw the policeman coming toward us from the other side.

"Annabelle, let's go," Mickey urged quietly, his hand on my shoulder.

"Claudia is not well, dear. And that's the truth of the matter. I'm sorry for your distress." Nancy pushed on the lavatory door and went in.

I started to follow her, but Mickey held me back. "No, you'll have that police officer charging in after you, and we'll be here for another several hours. Let's go, babe, this is all over."

I thought, *It can't be, not until I understand what the hell happened to Claudia.*

Mickey was firm in changing my direction to the street. We stood by the car, while Luis called the airline to make a plane reservation.

"I could use some more coffee, maybe a mocha with whipped cream." I scanned the street.

"Let's walk a bit. Settle ourselves. Find a café." Mickey got Luis' attention and we all started walking, Luis still on the phone.

We turned a corner a couple of blocks up and saw a sign for Stumptown Coffee Roasters, which looked promising.

But we didn't get there.

I stopped cold as a chilling thought hit me. *That wasn't Nancy's purse. It was Claudia's.*

I whirled around and ran back toward the police station with Mickey calling after me. I raced inside and into the ladies room, whirling around and bending over to look underneath the stall doors.

Mickey charged in after me along with two policemen, followed by Luis. "Annabelle! What the hell?!" Mickey yelled.

"Where is she?" I shouted.

"Miss, you need to calm down," advised one of the cops.

"Claudia's purse! She had Claudia's purse!"

Mickey thrust his arms straight out at me like he was going to stop me from talking or moving. "Babe, so what? What are you talking about?"

I grabbed his arms. "Mickey, Claudia would not give her purse to her mother if she was making her get out of the car, pointing a gun at her."

"Maybe Nancy just took it when she got out of the car..."

"No. You don't try to steal someone's purse when they're pointing a gun at you. Something is all wrong here."

The policeman approached us. "I am asking you once more to calm down, and I need you to come with me out of this bathroom."

Then Dawson ran in and stopped, surveying us. "What's the story?"

Mickey held my eyes. "Let's go back to the interview room and tell Dawson. It's not too late to find out from Nancy Bigelow what she's doing with that purse."

Dawson squinted at me. "Purse? What purse?"

"Claudia's. She has Claudia's purse."

"Well, fuck me."

Mickey jerked around toward him. "What."

"Nancy Bigelow. She just fainted, then came to and complained of nausea and sharp pains. She looked sick. She's on her way to the hospital in a medical transport van."

Luis walked over to the big trash can in the corner of the bathroom and peered in. He reached in and lifted something out.

Claudia's purse.

He handed it to Dawson, who opened it.

"Fuck me again."

He pulled out a gun and held it daintily, like it was a handkerchief, between his thumb and first finger.

"Holy moly, what is that?"

"A Colt Mustang," Mickey answered me.

"You gotta be kidding me. Nano, Bobcat, Mustang? Are gun manufacturers having way too much fun?"

Everyone ignored me.

"We need to stop that van," said Dawson. "You three, stay here. Sit down with Monroe and tell him about the purse."

"What's to tell? You're holding it right now!"

Dawson hurried out the bathroom door. "Just sit tight, okay? I'll ask Monroe to talk to you.

We followed him out into the hallway.

"We're not going to sit tight, are we?"

"*Amiga,* there is nothing we can do."

"We can find Claudia!"

Mickey sighed like he was exasperated. "Annabelle, there is no way we can do that. She could be anywhere, and they're looking for the Honda, and…"

"But I think I know where she is!"

Both of them stood with their arms folded. They looked like they were about to start a Blues Brothers routine. "*Amiga,* what do you mean?"

"The park. She's still at the park. I think Nancy left her there, and stashed the car at the airport."

"Why would Nancy hurt her daughter?"

"Don't you see, Mickey? It's always been Nancy, not Phillip. Nancy wrote that note. The handwriting is so neat and practiced like a rich woman's. The police didn't find it in Claudia's pocket when she was mugged. Nancy is the one Claudia wanted to shoot."

"Why wouldn't Phillip say something?"

I shook my head. "Maybe he doesn't know everything. Maybe he's trying to protect his wife and his daughter. Hell, I don't know, maybe he wants to shoot Nancy, too. Anyway, we have to go to the park!"

I started for the door, just as Monroe came around the corner. "Leaving?"

Mickey nodded. "Why don't you come with us? Annabelle has a theory about where Claudia is."

"No shit? Gee, I'm always ready to follow a well-meaning citizen around on a wild goose chase," he sneered.

"So take us in your car and bring an officer along if you want. What's the harm?"

Monroe paused. "Tell me about this theory."

I did.

The four of us left the station, got into Monroe's car, and he turned on the blinking lights and siren, wailing us all the way to Blue Lake Park.

Chapter Thirty-five

If you've never ridden in a detective's car with blinking lights flashing and a siren blaring, I highly recommend it. It's as exciting as an amusement park ride, even though when riding in an unmarked police vehicle, you should be in a situation that's anything but amusing. Nevertheless, it's a rush. I closed my eyes and imagined I was in an Aston Martin being driven by Daniel Craig a la James Bond, chasing after the bad guy who kidnapped Eva Green in *Casino Royale*. Then that made me think about the scene where she's sitting on the floor of the shower with her evening gown on, the water drenching her and she's upset, and Bond comes in and asks her if she's cold, and she says yes, and instead of turning off the shower, he sits down beside her in his tuxedo and hugs her, the water still running all over them.

That's one of my favorite romance scenes. Ever.

But now was not the time for romance. I was jolted from my escape-dream by Monroe taking a hard left into Blue Lake Park.

He parked and we jumped out, running to the place where Scranton got shot the previous night. "Where?" Monroe demanded.

All three men looked at me.

"I don't know! Somewhere close. We have to look!"

I sprinted toward the lake, while they all scurried off in other directions.

It's a small, pretty lake, and the sun was shining, so the water was sparkling. I saw some ducks paddling around, but no movement otherwise. I kept calling out for Claudia as I scurried along the lake.

I burst into the bathrooms, both women's and men's, but no luck. I rushed back out and called for her again.

Then I thought I heard something. A muffled sound. I turned around and ran to a pier jutting into the lake, stopped, and listened.

The same sound.

I saw a group of overturned paddleboats on the shore. I knew they were paddleboats because a sign said so. In warmer weather, they were available to rent for a leisurely jaunt around the lake.

"Claudia!" I yelled.

A knocking sound led me closer to the boats until it was clear. I tried to lift the boat, but it was too heavy.

"Mickey! Luis! Monroe! Over here!" I screamed. I crouched down close to the boat. "We're here, don't worry, Claudia. We'll get you out."

I was amazed she was alive, given that she spent the night on the ground, underneath a boat.

The three *amigos* came running and the four of us hoisted the boat up and over.

Claudia was curled up in a fetal position, shivering. Monroe quickly summoned an ambulance. Mickey and Luis lifted her up and brought her onto a grassy area, away from the lake. Luis took off his jacket and put it around her shoulders, while Mickey rubbed her hands.

Claudia looked blue. I mean it. I'd never seen an actual blue person before, other than in *Avatar,* but those bluebies weren't people, and frankly, I don't know what all the fuss was about with that movie anyway. But Claudia, she was in bad shape, judging by the hue of her face.

I squatted beside her. "Can you talk?"

She shook her head.

"Did your mother put you here?"

She nodded.

"Did you get the gun because you wanted to kill her?"

She shook her head.

Monroe stood behind me. "I've got a blanket from the car." He draped it around her and she clung to it like a baby clings to its mother.

Well, that is, if the baby's mother isn't Nancy Bigelow.

After we put Claudia in the ambulance, we all piled back into Monroe's car. He got a call on his cell before he turned the key in the ignition.

"Yeah, Dawson, what's up?"

Monroe didn't say another word before he hung up. But he did slam his hands against the steering wheel.

"Bad news?" Mickey asked.

"The Bigelow broad got away."

"How is that possible?" I asked, leaning forward over his shoulder, while Mickey gestured for me to sit back.

"It turns out we didn't use a medical transport vehicle. We had a rookie take her to the hospital in a patrol car. When they got to the hospital, he opened the back door, she got out, kicked him in his nuts, and bolted."

We were silent, taking in this unfortunate development.

"At least Claudia is in good hands now, and I am sure you will find Nancy," said Luis, full of optimism and what I guessed was anxiousness to go home and be done with all of this.

Monroe started the engine. "I don't know about that."

"The airport," Mickey said.

"What?" Monroe pulled out of the parking lot.

"Nancy will go to the airport to get her car. Has the airport security located it?"

Monroe nodded. "Dawson said yes."

"Did they leave it in place?"

Monroe nodded again. "Let's go."

I fastened my seat belt, and let the ride transport me once more to Daniel Craig–land, lights flashing, siren blaring, shower scene not suffering one bit from replay.

◇◇◇

The Portland Airport really is the best airport in the country, and I'm not the only one who thinks that. *Travel + Leisure* magazine has voted it so, at least in recent years. It's easy to get to, get around in, and get fed in. It has high-quality shops and a bright carpet, and live musicians play piano and guitar. It's an airport you could imagine going to just for fun.

This visit, of course, was for anything but fun. Monroe screeched into the parking garage and pulled his car to the side. We waited while he talked to a security guard, who had been warned of our approach. Dawson was on his way, too, along with a couple of patrol cars, but we were closer and got there first.

The Honda CRV was parked on the top level, and security cameras confirmed that it was still there. Monroe called Dawson and told him to get to the lot exit, while we wound our way up to the roof. We arrived, saw the car, and stopped several parking spaces away, where we could keep an eye on it.

We sat and waited, saying nothing, until I couldn't stand it any longer.

"Um, guys, I'm sorry, but I have to find a bathroom."

Monroe sighed, like I was a pain in the ass. And here I had been thinking we were on good terms now.

"Look, Detective, I'm sorry, but I have to go. I'll stay out of sight of the elevator and wait to get on before anyone gets off so that if Nancy..."

"You'll take the stairs."

"That's a lot of stairs."

"Annabelle, I think he's right. You have less chance of meeting Nancy on the stairs. Why don't I come with you?" Mickey unfastened his seat belt.

Monroe sighed again. "Sorry, no. I need all three of us here. If she comes out of the elevator bank over there," he pointed, "then I want the two of you on foot while I block her with my car so she can't back out in hers. We already know she's a runner. I'd like you and Luis to have a good chance of grabbing her, when she tries to bolt."

"Really? You think we need three men to take down a fifty-year-old woman?" Mickey sounded irritated.

"Mickey, it's okay. I'll be fine. And I have my phone. And my book." I smiled at him when he turned around.

"Be careful."

"Always!"

Luis took my hand. "*Amiga*, I suggest you do not come back up. Stay inside the airport until we let you know that this is over."

"Okey doke." I got out of the car and walked to the stairs.

So many stairs. Good thing I have a hardy bladder.

I started down at a clip, but I slowed to a walk soon, not wanting to bounce up and down too much. I mean, one should respect one's bladder and not challenge it unnecessarily.

I had made it down several flights when I heard footsteps coming the other way. *Not to panic,* I told myself. *Could be anyone. And don't think about that stairway fight in* Casino Royale. *That was bloody and scary and this is not that. This is not* Casino Royale *and you are not Daniel Craig, and Nancy is not coming up the stairs.*

I was right, two out of three.

Chapter Thirty-six

Nancy Bigelow was not a big woman. Not as tall as me and too thin, in my opinion. She's what I call rich thin. The rich thin choose to skip meals and eat salads with no dressing and drink chenin blanc because it has fewer calories. Well, Nancy drank more than that, but still. The rich thin have personal trainers and they've never worn a dress size bigger than four. Their favorite exercise is tennis because they get to wear little skirts to show off their legs. They aren't powerful servers, but they're good at the net. When they throw parties, they have them catered, even dinner for six. And they're eternally disappointed in their daughters, who are not athletic, prefer meatloaf over salmon, and have meaty calves that make knee boots a tight fit.

We stopped on the stairs, facing each other, me coming down, she coming up, and I thought, *I can take her. She's rich thin.*

But we didn't move. She was clearly surprised to see me, given the widening diameter of her eyes, and I was, at the very least, not happy to see her. I didn't know whether to chase her down the stairs, or let her pass and trip her when she did, or turn and run upstairs, leading her to my *compadres.*

I did none of these things.

I sat down, pulled out my phone, and speed-dialed Mickey. "She's here," I said, when he picked up. "On the stairs."

I dropped the phone back in my purse and smiled at Nancy. "We got you."

And then, swear to God, she did the impossible.

She pulled out a gun.

Number three, by my count.

She pointed it at me and said, "Stand up."

I didn't. "What is *that* one called, a Panther?" It was black and sleek.

"Stand up."

I stayed seated. "Where in the world did you get another gun, Nancy?"

"That would be from me," answered a voice from further down the stairwell. Approaching footsteps brought another woman into my view.

It was Greta.

How in the hell did Nancy and Greta know each other?

"Wow. Greta." I managed to look cool, or at least, I hoped I did. "Great to see you again, and did you know your name is an anagram for 'great'? I mean, that's truly great." My knees were starting to knock, and I was ready to let my bladder loose.

"She called Mickey, her boyfriend," Nancy informed Greta.

"Fiancé." I corrected her. "You're the first to know."

"Shut up. Get up. And come with us." Greta walked up to me and grabbed my T-shirt, pulling it toward her. I resisted, but Nancy got closer with the Panther. So I stood up.

"Where to?"

"This level." They shoved me out onto the fourth floor of the parking garage.

"I have to pee."

"Too bad," they replied in unison.

"Mickey's on his way with a zillion cops."

"So what." They were sounding like a Greek chorus.

"He'll find us on level four." My phone was still on. I hoped Mickey was listening and that he could hear me.

Then I saw the skybridge. The walkway over the roadway that leads into the terminal. And I thought, *Nancy isn't going to shoot me. Not in this garage, with people nearby. She's smarter than that.*

But then I thought, *Greta is bad ass.*

Nancy had the gun in my back. Greta had her arm looped through mine, like we were in love, or sisters, or both. With Greta, anything was possible.

"Skybridge?" I asked, loudly.

They walked me over to it and just as we entered, a group of high-schoolers was exiting, taking up a lot of room as groups of high-schoolers will do, which made the three of us have to shift position. Greta turned so that our backs were against the railing. Nancy put her gun inside her jacket so it wouldn't be noticeable.

I saw my opportunity.

"Hey! Anyone know where the closest ladies room is?" I yelled.

The kids giggled and one pointed toward the terminal "You'll see signs, up ahead, take the escalator…"

I didn't hear the rest. I had brought attention to us, and that's all I needed to twist myself out of Greta's hold and slap her across the face.

"Whoa, lady! WTF?" a boy in an Oregon Ducks cap shouted, but the kids just stood there.

I ran.

Greta ran after me, followed by Nancy, I assumed.

Like I said before, I can run, but it was a shame that Greta could, too.

She caught up and tackled me, and we both fell to the floor. My purse went flying and I saw my cell phone skitter away. Nancy rushed to us while Greta was getting to her feet.

I grabbed Nancy's ankle, and she fell, the gun following the path of my phone.

Nancy screamed, and I scrambled to my feet, only to see Greta coming at me.

I was leaning against the railing, and at the last minute I dodged her. The railing hit her hard in her solar plexus.

It knocked the wind out of her, I guess, because she gasped for breath.

Then she pulled out a knife.

There was nothing I could do but save myself.

I ducked, took hold of her legs, and tossed her over the side of the skybridge.

Greta wasn't rich thin. She landed hard, right on top of a bright yellow Fiat 500. I always liked those cars, but I'll never get one after watching Greta's torso land splat on the roof, her head falling over the windshield like she had just dropped in to say hello. The car screeched to a halt and a young couple jumped out, screaming.

I heard other screams behind me, and people running.

I turned around to find Nancy.

She was gone.

Most of the teenagers were still standing there, gaping at me. "I called 911," said the Ducks cap kid.

"Good. Thanks. Look, when they get here, tell them I'm in the ladies room, okay? Just sit tight. I'll be right back."

And with that, I stumbled my way into the terminal and saw two things that made me feel a lot better.

One was Mickey, who was holding a gun on Nancy Bigelow, who was sitting on the floor, her hands behind her head. A crowd had gathered, and security guards were approaching.

The other was a sign for the restrooms.

Mickey saw me. "Annabelle," he called to me. "Sweetheart, are you all right?"

I thought I was, really. I thought I was. But the adrenalin rush that gave me the power to flip Greta over the handrail had abandoned me faster than a politician's promise, as soon as Mickey called me "sweetheart." I looked at him holding the gun on Nancy, and that coupled with the vision of Greta splayed on top of that cute little Fiat made my knees give way to the floor.

"Babe!"

I gave a weak wave, and then damn it all, if I didn't pee, right then and there.

Chapter Thirty-seven

There are worse things than peeing in your pants in a busy airport terminal with your boyfriend—I mean, fiancé—holding a gun on a woman and watching you. I mean, we were alive and safe and we got the bad guys. Um, girls. Whatever.

Mickey got to me quickly and figured out what had happened right away, when I said, "I haven't done that since preschool."

"Hey, it's okay. Don't even think about it. No one can see. You've got your blue jeans on. Here." He took off his sports jacket which came down far enough to cover my crotch, when I stood. "You're okay. Holy shit, Annabelle, you're not okay. You're unbelievable. I saw you flip Greta over the rail." He put his arms around me and we stood there for a while, until Luis and Monroe joined us.

"I need to get cleaned up," I murmured.

Mickey said something to the guys, and then walked me to the ladies room. "I'm going to stand right by the door. You take as much time as you need." He kissed my cheek.

I went in the stall for handicapped women, which has its own private sink. I took off my pants and undies and rinsed them both, tidied myself up the best I could, and dried everything at least a little with paper towels. I got dressed in my damp clothes and flashed on the beginning of my trip christened by Scranton's wine. Must have been an omen.

I met Mickey outside.

"Better?" he asked.

"Yes." I buttoned his jacket. "Police station?"

"Our home away from home, these days. Monroe's going to take us."

We returned to the skybridge, where I saw that Nancy was in cuffs and being led away by uniforms. "Mickey, do we even know what the hell she was doing?"

"Most of it. I'll fill you in on the ride downtown. Phillip started talking, and I bet Nancy will spill her guts."

"Hey."

"Hey."

"Do I smell like a homeless person?"

He inhaled an exaggerated sniff. "No, you smell like someone who lives with a man who adores you."

"Hmm. What does that smell like, exactly? Coconut? Lemon? Scotch?"

Mickey stopped and took me in his arms. "Passion fruit."

"Does that even have a scent?"

He kissed me. "Oh, yes, indeed. It has an intoxicating aroma, and I'm surprised that men don't follow you everywhere, sniffing."

I rolled my eyes. "Mickey, you don't know crap about botany or fruits or trees or any of it. You're making this up."

He smiled. "Maybe, maybe not. Look it up. Either way, I know that I'd like to smell you for the rest of my life."

"For that, I am eternally grateful."

This is what I learned in the car going back to the station, and later on that day.

Claudia was going to recover. She was suffering from exposure, but her vitals were good.

Phillip told the police that Claudia was his daughter, but not Nancy's. He had an affair years back, and talked his wife into taking the baby when his mistress said she was going to put her up for adoption. Ever since, Nancy has had it out for Claudia.

"But he said he didn't realize how much," added Monroe.

Phillip was holding back information all along in a misguided effort to help Claudia. He found out that she was planning on picking up the gun at the airport because she actually told him.

"Why didn't he tell the police?"

"Fathers think they can protect their daughters. He called on Scranton instead, fixing it for him to land at PDX at about the same time as the drop." Monroe was driving the speed limit, with no lights and no sirens, which was a welcome relief.

Scranton didn't get the backpack, because I got it. He figured I did, which was why he was stalking us.

More misguided efforts.

Nancy was trying to prove that Claudia was psychotic. She had been pretty good at convincing Claudia of the same thing, setting up situations that made Claudia feel crazy, like moving furniture around in the house, and making phone calls but insisting they weren't made. Stuff like that.

Wesley was the one who helped Claudia see the light. Turns out he was a caring boyfriend. He didn't hit her, ever. Nancy made that up.

Nancy not only resented Claudia because of Phillip's affair, she didn't want Claudia to have access to the trust fund that Phillip set up for her, managed by Scranton. She didn't want Claudia to have anything.

Not even a mother.

Those pills I found? Nancy told Claudia in the suite that she had to start taking them. They weren't a real prescription. Greta got them for Nancy and faked the label. Claudia refused the pills and got into it heavy with her mother, so heavy that Phillip was alarmed. He was starting doubt Nancy's insistence that Claudia was crazy. So he got her out of the suite and took her to the movies, to try to calm her down and get her away from Nancy for a while.

Phillip, by the way, never did anything sick to his daughter. He was simply a clueless, absent father who was severely delusional in his estimation of his own sex appeal.

Greta wasn't dead, but she was as good as dead. Once her broken bones and fractured skull healed, she'd spend the rest of her crummy life in jail.

Oh yeah, Nancy and Greta? When Nancy heard about the Uptown Billiards Club and Greta and the gun—from little ole big-mouth me—she went there to track down Greta, who just happened to be grabbing some merchandise from the cellar when Nancy got there. Nancy wanted a getaway plan, in case her scheme to portray Claudia as a nutcase was revealed. She promised Greta a ride out of town. Greta had a burner phone. That's how Nancy got in touch with her before heading to the airport.

As for Claudia, was she going to kill her mother? Or, even worse, did she feel so crazy that she was considering suicide?

I didn't know, but I wanted to find out.

Monroe and Dawson thanked Mickey, Luis, and me for our help. As we were leaving the station, Monroe stopped me.

"Annabelle."

"Yes?"

"Nice work. You ever think about joining the force?"

I smiled. "What, and leave these two hunkadorises for the likes of you? No way. Besides, I hate guns."

He gave me a nod and turned away.

"Monroe."

"Yeah?" He turned back.

"Watch out for those Cheese Doodles."

Reflexively, he touched his lip, but it was clean.

Mom and I went to see Claudia the next morning. She was sitting up in bed and looking the best I had seen her. She even smiled at us.

"Hi."

Mom took her hand. "Claudia, how are you feeling?"

"Better. Much better."

I took her other hand. "We know everything now, about your mother."

"I'll be all right. Wesley will take care of me. I'll be all right." She was repeating it, like she needed to convince herself.

"Claudia, maybe you've already told the police, but why did you want that gun?"

"I was so scared, of my mother, of myself. I told myself that I needed it for protection. But when I realized I didn't have it, I didn't want it anymore. It was the craziest thing I had ever done, and it was the final thing that convinced me my mother was screwing with my head."

"So, why did you take me out to Blue Lake, pointing that gun at me? You still might be charged with kidnapping, you know." I didn't know this, but it sounded reasonable.

"I'm sorry about that. I wanted to make my mother confess what she was up to, if in fact, she was doing everything that I thought she was doing. I wanted you to be a witness. And I really did think I might shoot her, which is why I picked Blue Lake Park, but I also thought that if I did, I'd want you to either arrest me or stop me."

I frowned. "Arrest you? Claudia, I'm not a cop. I'm not even a detective. You could have just asked me to go with you."

She shook her head. "Mom wouldn't have gone along with it unless I acted mental, which is what she wanted you and everyone else to think."

"So, now it seems that Nancy shot Loren Scranton?"

"Yeah. When you ran, Mother got the gun away from me. She shot Scranton, then she shoved me under that paddle boat, since I was a witness. She told me Scranton would die and so would I, and she'd fix it so that Dad would get blamed, it being his gun. I couldn't get out. I tried digging under the boat, but the ground was too hard. I wore myself out until I passed out."

"How did Nancy lift the paddle boat, to shove you under? The thing must weigh a hundred pounds!"

Claudia's eyes teared up. "It was tilted, with one edge on a boulder. She made me crawl under it, and then she rocked the boat little by little until it slammed down on the ground. She's stronger than you think."

Rich strong, I thought.

Mom reached over and grabbed a tissue for Claudia and handed it to her. "Lucky you were positioned in the right place, or it could have done some real damage."

Claudia blew her nose. "Yeah. I'm going to be in the hospital for a couple of days, the doctor said. They want to run more tests, said I was probably still recovering from being attacked in the garden."

"It did seem like they released you from the other hospital awfully soon after waking up from that coma." Mom fluffed up her pillows.

"Mother insisted."

I traded looks with Mom. I guessed she was thinking the same thing I was. *What a fucking psycho freakass sicko shitwad mother.* Or words to that effect.

I unclenched my jaw. "Just one more question, and then we'll leave you alone. How did you get your father's gun?"

"Mother had it. She brought it from Seattle. I found it at the hotel suite."

"I think your father might be around more than usual, to look out for you," Mom said.

"Maybe. He wasn't sure if I was crazy or not." She paused. "He's gone most of the time."

I squeezed her hand. "He doesn't know much about being a father, I'm afraid. Look, stay away from guns, okay? And go back to school. I think the law will go easy on you. Now you know you're not crazy. Just ended up with a bad mother."

She thanked us for coming, and we left.

Outside of the hospital I stopped and hugged Mom. "I love you."

She hugged me back. "Oh, for fuck's sake, Bea, of course you do."

Chapter Thirty-eight

Luis caught a plane back to Las Vegas that afternoon. We were sorry to see him leave, but we knew he had been away from his beloved pregnant Ruby a lot longer than he had expected. Mickey paid for his plane ticket (first class, of course, even though it was a short flight) and told him he had opened a savings account in "Baby Maldonado's" name in New York, in appreciation for his help.

Luis gave him a man hug. "*Mi hermano, gracias. Siempre.*"

Luis hugged me, too. "*Amiga,* you are all right?"

I kissed his cheek. "I am *mucho* all right, Luis."

Mom planted a kiss on his cheek. "Come back and see us, with Ruby and the baby. Or we'll see you in New York, soon, I hope!"

"I will look forward to that, Sylvia. And, Annabelle," he turned to me. "I still like your mother." He winked.

Dad shook his hand and hugged him. "Good to have you part of the family."

Luis choked up a little on that one.

As we walked Luis out to the curb where the cab was waiting, Sal and Drew were sweeping their porch and hanging pumpkin lights, I figured in anticipation of Thanksgiving, still three weeks away. They waved energetically. "Luis! Come back!"

Luis waved and got in the cab.

As it drove away, Sal yelled to us, "Drinks later?"

Mom answered. "Six. Our house. Bring cheeses!"

And back inside we went.

Mickey and I were lying on top of the bed fully clothed, thinking we were going to nap, but unable to. A jumble of thoughts raced around my head. I had two issues to discuss with him, and I wasn't sure where to start.

But I did.

"Guns."

"Huh?"

"Guns, Mickey. You know they make me uncomfortable. I read about people shooting other people by accident all the time. I guess I'm afraid I could do the same thing if I had a gun."

"We don't have to talk about this now. But you already have one. If you don't want to carry it, you don't have to."

I propped myself up on an elbow and looked at him. "Chopstick, pool cue, book, purse, strong like ox, and fleet of foot. Those are my current weapons of choice."

"You forgot dental floss, your preferred binding material." His eyes twinkled.

"Don't make fun of me, Mickey, I mean it."

"I'm not. I'm in awe of your resourcefulness." He propped himself up on an elbow, too, so that we were facing each other. "You're the strongest woman I've ever met, and I don't mean muscles, though you've got them. I mean will. I mean temperament. I mean guts."

"Even though my knees buckle and I pee in my pants?"

He fell onto his back and snorted. "I've seen seasoned cops lose it in far worse ways than that."

"That's a relief. So, anyway, back to the gun. My gun."

"It's not an issue, like I said. It can stay in the closet."

"Nope."

He peered at me with his best Mickey Paxton squint. "Nope?"

"I'm going to learn how to use it. I don't want to be afraid of it, and if I'm going to do anything other than dumpster dive, there may very well be situations confronted by Asta Investigations where I'll need it. You and Luis might not be there every time I'm in danger. I'm good at putting up a fight, and I'm good at thinking on my feet, but I'm not going run away from that gun. Not if I want to get my detective's license someday. Not if we're really going to be equal partners."

Mickey beamed. "You amaze me. Come here." He reached for me.

"Not yet." I sat up. "Back to dumpster diving, I haven't done that yet. Will it be my job and not yours or Luis'?"

He looked amused. "We'll dive together, how about that? Your talents still have much to reveal, methinks, but perhaps you were a little hasty when you put that 'DDS' on your business card."

"Oh, I'm probably good at it, don't worry."

He chuckled and reached for me again, but I shook my head. "So, what about the other thing?"

"What other thing?"

"That other thing we said we were going to do." I bit my lip.

His mouth twitched like he was trying not to smile. "Oh, you mean get married?"

I nodded.

"What about it?"

"Was that a real proposal?"

"Was that a real 'yes'?"

"I asked you first."

He pulled me down on top of him and kissed me hard. "It was the realest thing I've ever asked, anyone."

"Okay, then. Yes, for real." I grinned.

We kissed again, then curled up on the bed. We were soon fast asleep.

Wine and cheese with Mom and Dad and Sal and Drew was jolly and lighthearted. We examined possible tablecloths for the bakery, and curtain fabric, and we tasted a new bread recipe from a warm loaf they had just pulled out of the oven and sliced before coming over. I was nestled close to Mickey on the couch, thinking about how we would get along in thirty years, hoping our marriage would bear some resemblance to my parents'.

I picked up the catalog of handguns that was still on the coffee table and waved it at Sal and Drew. "So, tell me, you guys, why do you have a gun?"

Sal took it from me. "Honestly, we got it when that wacko father was sending homophobic nasty letters, accusing Drew of corrupting his son and threatening to set him on fire."

"Holy shit, you left that part out of the story before."

"None of us needed to hear any more drama that night, Sylvia sweetheart. Anyway, we've never used it, but we know how. So, are you and Jeff going to get one?"

Before Mom could answer, Dad piped up. "No. It was a fleeting curiosity. Not for us."

"If you change your mind, Dad, Mickey can advise you."

Both of my parents jerked like they had spasms fire up their backs. "Muffinhead?"

"I'm going to learn how to shoot. I want to get my license to be a detective. If you decide to get a gun, you'll get no judgment from me."

Sal rolled the catalog and stuck it in his jacket pocket. "Brava! Let's drink to that!"

I squeezed Mickey's hand and exhaled deeply.

Mom pointed her finger at Mickey. "That gun in the closet in New York, the Nanette, or whatever it's called, will Annabelle be okay…?"

Mickey cut her off. "No worries, Sylvia. I won't let her anywhere near it by herself until she's a veritable Annie Oakley."

She sat back. "I told you, honey, he's a goddamn keeper."

"I learn so much from you, Mom." We raised our glasses to each other.

"I'm astonished. Simply astonished." Dad cracked the second bottle of wine and poured it. When Mickey stood, his glass in hand, I thought he was going to make *the* announcement, but instead he thanked them all for their hospitality and wished for calmer days ahead. We all sipped.

Then I sat up like a shot. "It's Tuesday!"

"Yes, darling," Mom said, "it happens each week."

"'Rawhide' is on at The Rowdy Yeats! Let's go!"

After explaining this to Sal and Drew, we put on coats and got ready to pile into two cars. Mickey stopped us. "I'd like to ride with Jeff. Sylvia, okay if you and Annabelle ride with Sal and Drew?"

Mom looked puzzled, but said sure.

I traded a knowing glance with Mickey, my heart pounding like the Mumford & Sons' bass drum.

◇◇◇

Perry, forgiving guy that he was, welcomed us as we sat at the bar. A young Clint Eastwood was on the screen behind the bar, with subtitles revealing the dialogue. We ordered drinks, and I got up to play some pool. I love "Rawhide," but I felt the need to move around a bit and feel, well, rowdy, in a good way.

Mom got up to play with me. I racked up the balls and offered her the break. She positioned the cue ball and blasted it into the triangle of stripes and solids. One of each fell in.

"You're solids, that's what fell first. Thanks for the freebie!" I took a sip of my bourbon.

Then, honest to God, I sank all of the stripes. I had never played a better game of pool in my life, even better than when I finished off the table at the Uptown Billiards Club. I was making shots that made no sense. It was like I was channeling the goddess of pool, making every great shot that had ever been made on a pool table ever. I was batting a hundred.

My family and friends had stopped watching the screen and were watching me. It was exhilarating.

When I sent the eight ball careening into the far corner pocket, they gave me some whoops and a round of applause.

Mickey stood up and held up his glass. "That's my fiancée!"

Mom dropped her pool cue and it clattered on the floor. "No shit?! You two are getting married?"

Sal and Drew cheered while Dad took me in his arms. "Mickey asked for my blessing on the way over. He's a gem, Bea, and he knows you are, too."

I couldn't help it. I let it all go, sobbing into my father's chest, so happy and exhausted and full of love that Dad practically had to hold me up. Mom came to me and pulled me to her, telling me that she loved me and that Mickey was the fucking greatest man I could ever marry.

Then I was in Mickey's arms, feeling like I was being passed around like a precious child, only when I looked into his eyes, those eyes that are deeper than an Ingmar Bergman movie, I didn't feel like a child. I felt like a wife, a partner, and an equal.

I couldn't have been happier than if I had just pitched a game-winning grand slam. No bullmarkey.

To receive a free catalog of Poisoned Pen Press titles, please provide your name, address, and email address in one of the following ways:

Phone: 1-800-421-3976
Facsimile: 1-480-949-1707
Email: info@poisonedpenpress.com
Website: www.poisonedpenpress.com

Poisoned Pen Press
6962 E. First Ave. Ste 103
Scottsdale, AZ 85251